Praise for
MAJ SJÖWALL and
PER WAHLÖÖ

"Ingenious. . . . Their mysteries don't just read well; they reread even better. . . . The writing is lean, with mournful undertones."
—*The New York Times*

"Magically successful, a series of crime novels you shouldn't miss." —*Minneapolis Tribune*

"Sjöwall and Wahlöö are the best writers of police procedurals in the world." —*The Birmingham Post*

"These books are cream to crime buffs, a growing cult." —*Cosmopolitan*

"The husband-wife combination forms a superb storytelling team." —*El Paso Times*

"In the field of international 'roman policier,' or police story, these Swedish writers have few equals. Perhaps Georges Simenon is their only competitor." —*Newark News*

MAJ SJÖWALL and
PER WAHLÖÖ

THE MAN WHO
WENT UP IN SMOKE

Maj Sjöwall and her husband, Per Wahlöö, wrote ten Martin Beck mysteries. Mr. Wahlöö, who died in 1975, was a reporter for several Swedish newspapers and magazines and wrote numerous radio and television plays, film scripts, short stories, and novels. Maj Sjöwall is a poet. The books, together known as "The Story of Crime," remain one of the greatest series of crime stories ever written.

THE MARTIN BECK MYSTERY SERIES
by
MAJ SJÖWALL and
PER WAHLÖÖ

Roseanna
The Man Who Went Up in Smoke
The Man on the Balcony
The Laughing Policeman
The Fire Engine That Disappeared
Murder at the Savoy
The Abominable Man
The Locked Room
Cop Killer
The Terrorists

THE MAN WHO WENT UP IN SMOKE

THE MAN WHO WENT UP IN SMOKE

A MARTIN BECK MYSTERY

MAJ SJÖWALL and
PER WAHLÖÖ

Translated from the Swedish by JOAN TATE

Vintage Crime/Black Lizard
Vintage Books • A Division of Random House, Inc. • New York

SECOND VINTAGE CRIME/BLACK LIZARD EDITION, OCTOBER 2008

The Library of Congress Cataloging-in-Publication Data:
Sjöwall, Maj, 1935–
[Mannen som gick upp i rök. English]
The man who went up in smoke / by Maj Sjöwall and Per Wahlöö ;
translated from the Swedish by Joan Tate.
—1st Vintage Crime/Black Lizard ed.
p. cm.
I. Wahlöö, Per, 1926–1975. II. Title. III. Series.
PT9876.29.J63M313 1993
839.7'374—dc20 92-50694

Vintage ISBN: 978-0-307-39048-6

www.vintagebooks.com

Printed in the United States of America
10 9 8 7 6 5 4 3 2 1

INTRODUCTION

I first went to America in 1979. I had to buy another holdall to bring home the books. Discovering dedicated mystery booksellers was a bit like going to heaven without having to die first. There were so many crime writers whose books were available in the U.S. only—ironically, some of them British—and in those pre-Internet days, the only apparent way to acquire them was to physically go there and buy them. Which I did. In industrial quantities.

Among the books in the holdall were ten paperbacks in the black livery of Vintage Press. They comprised a decalogue of crime novels written by the Swedish husband-and-wife team Maj Sjöwall and Per Wahlöö. They'd been on my must-read list since I'd read about them in Julian Symonds's definitive overview of the genre, *Bloody Murder*. He said, "They might come under the heading of 'Police Novels' except that the authors are more interested in the philosophical implications of crime than in straightforward police routine . . . [They] are markedly individual and very good." I suppose it was a bit of a gamble to buy all ten on the recommendation alone. But it's a gamble I've never regretted.

Reading the Martin Beck series with twenty-first-century eyes, it's almost impossible to grasp how revolutionary they felt when they first appeared almost forty years ago. So many of the elements that have become integral to the point of cliché in the police procedural subgenre started life in these ten novels. So many of the features we take for granted and sigh over in a world-weary way have their roots in the work of a couple of journalists turned crime writers.

In the mid-sixties, when Sjöwall and Wahlöö started writing, there were plenty of examples of the police procedural novel around. Going back to the golden age of the 1930s, Ngaio Marsh's Inspector Alleyn and Freeman Wills Crofts's Inspector French were among those who led the way, but they were followed in a steady stream by the likes of J. J. Marric's Gideon and, on the other side of the Atlantic, Ed McBain.

What these examples of *roman policier* have in common is that they are wedded to the status quo. Their world is divided into black and white, good and evil, right and wrong, with no uncomfortable intervening gray area. Bad men—and very occasionally bad women—do bad things and thus are bound to come to a bad end. Their police officers are honorable, upstanding family men who believe in the rule of law and the delivery of justice by their own hands. A bent cop is almost unthinkable; an incompetent one only a little less so.

And while the star of the series may have a sidekick, invariably less gifted and often more brawny, little more than lip service is paid to the rest of the squad, whose legwork goes mostly unrecognized. (McBain later became an exception to this, but in the earlier 87th Precinct novels Steve Carella is invariably center-stage.) The police procedural was home to a singular hero. There was no room to share the limelight.

The books of Sjöwall and Wahlöö are different. Although they are generally referred to as the Martin Beck novels, they're not really about an individual. They're ensemble pieces.

Beck is not some solo maverick who operates with flagrant disregard for the rules and thinly disguised contempt for the lesser mortals who surround him. Nor is he a phenomenal genius blessed with so extraordinary a talent that mere mortals can only stand back in amazement as he leads them unerringly to the solution to the baffling mystery. He's not glamorous either. Not the scion of some high-society family, not the husband of an acclaimed portrait painter, nor the flamboyant solver of baffling mysteries with an upward flick of a single eyebrow.

No, Martin Beck is none of these things. He's a driven, middle-aged dyspeptic whose marriage slowly disintegrates during the series. Not because of some cataclysmic infidelity or clash of belief systems, but rather because of the quiet desperation that builds between two people who once loved each other but now have nothing in common but their children and their address.

He's also something of an idealist whose job forces him to confront the gulf between what should exist in an ideal world and what exists in actuality. His awareness of that gap colors his life, making him depressed and sometimes fatalistic about whether what he does can ever make a difference.

But more than this, he is part of a team, each member of which is a fully realized character. His strengths and weaknesses are balanced by those of his colleagues. He relies on them as they rely on him. This is a world where ideas are kicked around, where no individual has the monopoly on shafts of brilliant insight. Nor are the repetitive tedious tasks carried out offstage by minor minions. Both action and routine are shared between Beck and his underlings. Friendships and enmities are equally tested in the course of the ten books, and everyone is portrayed as an individual who has virtues and vices in distinct measure.

Of itself, that would be enough to mark these books out as different from the run of the mill. But Sjöwall and Wahlöö add other elements to the mix which demonstrate the uniqueness of their vision.

Their plots, for example, are second to none, both in terms of structure and subject. Sometimes it's the starting point which is surprising, a seemingly eccentric moment that leads cunningly to the heart of something much darker. Sometimes it's the choice of the underlying issue which confounds us; lulled into thinking we're getting one kind of story, we suddenly find ourselves in a very different place. Wherever their stories take us, Sjöwall and Wahlöö find ways to catch the reader on the back foot, making us reassess our take on the world.

Then there is that aspect that Julian Symonds picked on so astutely—their interest in the philosophical aspects of crime.

These days, it is a given that the crime novel is capable of shining a light on society, of illuminating us to ourselves. At its best, the contemporary crime novel tells us how our society works, revealing its social strata and its patterns. It can strip away the surfaces, leaving the malign and the benign exposed, and it can use both characters and story lines to excoriate us for our sins.

But back when Sjöwall and Wahlöö started writing, those jobs were left to literary novelists. Crime writers were only supposed to entertain. The Swedish duo demonstrated that there was a different way to write about murder. Through the eyes of Martin Beck and his colleagues, they held a mirror up to Swedish society at a time when the ideals of the welfare state were beginning to buckle under the realities of everyday life. They write unsparingly and unswervingly about social ills and problems, but they never forget that they are writing novels, not polemics. They dress up their social concerns in fast-moving storytelling, never losing sight of the need to keep their readers engaged.

The end product, though serious in intent, is far from gloomy. Sjöwall and Wahlöö are blessed with the gift of humor. It manifests itself in the sly, dark wit of Beck, but also in the knock-about farce that erupts from time to time, generally through the characters of Kristiansson and Kvant, a pair of patrol cops who are as stupid as they are unlucky. Their slapstick interludes are as funny to the reader as they are frustrating to the detectives. Before Sjöwall and Wahlöö, such a pair of Keystone Kops would have been unthinkable, undermining as they do the seriousness of police investigation and bringing it squarely into the realm of normal human behavior.

In many respects, however, *The Man Who Went Up in Smoke* is an exception to the rest of the novels. It takes place mostly outside Sweden, in Budapest, at a time when the cold war was still an unnerving backdrop to everyday life. For much of the book, Beck is on his own in a strange land, without back-up and without any visceral understanding of the society he's trying to operate in. His investigation into the disappearance of a Swedish journalist seems to run into brick walls at every turn, growing more and more baffling with each successive revelation.

Soon we come to understand that Beck can't crack the case on his own. He has to draw on help from both his colleagues at home and from unexpected sources in Budapest before the pieces can finally fall into place, revealing a truth that manages to be both banal and original.

Sjöwall and Wahlöö won the Mystery Writers of America's Edgar Award for Best Novel in 1971 with *The Laughing Policeman*. It remains the only novel in translation ever to have won the award. To me, that's not particularly surprising. I guarantee if you read their books, you'll end up agreeing with me. And with all the other crime writers who know only too well how much we owe to that pair of Swedish journalists turned novelists.

—*Val McDermid*

THE MAN
WHO WENT UP
IN SMOKE

1

The room was small and shabby. There were no curtains and the view outside consisted of a gray fire wall, a few rusty armatures and a faded advertisement for margarine. The center pane of glass in the left half of the window was gone and had been replaced by a roughly cut piece of cardboard. The wallpaper was floral, but so discolored by soot and seeping moisture that the pattern was scarcely visible. Here and there it had come away from the crumbling plaster, and in several places there had been attempts to repair it with adhesive strips and wrapping paper.

There were a heating stove, six pieces of furniture and a picture in the room. In front of the stove stood a cardboard box of ashes and a dented aluminum coffee pot. The end of the bed faced the stove and the bedclothes consisted of a thick layer of old newspapers, a ragged quilt and a striped pillow. The picture was of a naked blonde standing beside a marble balustrade, and it was hanging to the right of the stove so that the person lying in the bed could see it before he fell asleep and immediately when he woke up. Someone appeared to have enlarged the woman's nipples and genitals with a pencil.

In the other part of the room, nearest to the window, stood a round table and two wooden chairs, of which one had lost its back. On the table were three empty vermouth bottles, a soft-drink bottle and two coffee cups, among other things. The ash tray had been turned upside down and among the cigarette butts, bottle tops and dead matches lay a few dirty sugar lumps, a small penknife with its blades open, and a piece of sausage. A third coffee cup had fallen to the floor and had broken. Face down on the worn linoleum, between the table and the bed, lay a dead body.

In all probability this was the same person who had improved upon the picture and tried to mend the wallpaper with strips of adhesive and wrapping paper. It was a man and he was lying with his legs close together, his elbows pressed against his ribs and his hands drawn up toward his head, as if in an effort to protect himself. The man was wearing a woolen vest and frayed trousers. On his feet were ragged woolen socks. A large sideboard had been tipped over him, obscuring his head and half the top part of his body. The third wooden chair had been thrown down beside the corpse. Its seat was bloodstained and on the top of the back handprints were clearly visible. The floor was covered with pieces of glass. Some of them had come from the glass doors of the sideboard, others from a half-shattered wine bottle which had been thrown onto a heap of dirty underclothes by the wall. What was left of the bottle was covered with a thin skin of dried blood. Someone had drawn a white circle around it.

Of its kind, the picture was almost perfect, taken by the best wide-angle lens the police possessed and in an artificial light that gave an etched sharpness to every detail.

Martin Beck put down the photograph and magnifying glass, got up and went across to the window. Outside it was full Swedish summer. And more than that. It was hot. On the grass of Kristineberg Park a couple of girls were sunbathing in bikinis. They were lying flat on their backs with their legs apart and their arms stretched outward away from their bodies. They were young and thin, or slim as they say, and they could do this with a certain grace. When he focused sharply, he even recognized them as two office girls from his own department. So it was already past twelve. In the morning they put on their bathing suits, cotton dresses and sandals and went to work. In the lunch hour they took off their dresses and went out and lay in the park. Practical.

Dejectedly, he recalled that soon he would have to leave all this and move over to the south police headquarters in the rowdy neighborhood around Västberga Allé.

Behind him he heard someone fling open the door and come into the room. He did not need to turn around to know who it was. Stenström. Stenström was still the youngest in the department and after him there would presumably be a whole generation of detectives who did not knock on doors.

"How's it going?" he said.

"Not so well," said Stenström. "When I was there fifteen minutes ago he was still flatly denying everything."

Martin Beck turned around, went back to his desk and once again looked at the photo of the scene of the crime. On the ceiling above the newspaper mattress, the ragged quilt and the striped pillow, there was an old patch of dampness. It looked like a sea horse. With a little good will it could have been a mermaid. He wondered if the man on the floor had had that much imagination.

"It doesn't matter," said Stenström officiously. "We'll get him on the technical evidence."

Martin Beck made no reply. Instead he pointed at the thick report Stenström had put down on his desk and said, "What's that?"

"The record of the interrogation from Sundbyberg."

"Take the miserable thing away. Starting tomorrow I'm on my holiday. Give it to Kollberg. Or to anybody you damn please."

Martin Beck took the photograph and went up one flight of stairs, opened a door and found himself with Kollberg and Melander.

It was much warmer in there than in his room, presumably because the windows were closed and the curtains drawn. Kollberg and the suspect were sitting opposite each other at the table, quite still. Melander, a tall man, was standing by the window, his pipe in his mouth and his arms folded. He was looking steadily at the suspect. On a chair by the door sat a police guard in uniform trousers and a light-blue shirt. He was balancing his cap on his right knee. No one said anything and the only moving thing was the reel of the tape recorder. Martin Beck situated himself to one side and just behind Kollberg and joined in the general silence. A wasp could be heard bouncing against the window behind the curtains. Kollberg had taken off his jacket and unbuttoned his shirt, but even so, his shirt was soaked with sweat between his plump shoulder blades. The wet patch slowly changed shape and spread downward in a line along his spine.

The man on the other side of the table was small, with thinning hair. He was slovenly dressed and the fingers gripping the arms of his chair were uncared-for, with bitten, dirty nails. His face was thin and sickly, with weak evasive lines around his mouth. His chin was trembling slightly and his eyes seemed cloudy and watery. The man hunched up and two tears fell down his cheeks.

"Uh-huh," said Kollberg gloomily. "You hit him on the head with the bottle, then, until it broke?"

The man nodded.

"Then you went on hitting him with the chair as he lay on the floor. How many times?"

"Don't know. Not many. Quite a lot though."

"I can imagine. And then you tipped the sideboard over him and left the room. What did the third one of you do in the meantime? This Ragnar Larsson? Didn't he try to interfere; I mean, stop you?"

"No, he didn't do anything. He just let it go on."

"Don't start lying again now."

"He was asleep. He'd passed out."

"Try to speak a little louder, all right?"

"He was lying on the bed, asleep. He didn't notice anything."

"No, not until he came to and then he went to the police.

Well, so far it's clear. But there's one thing I still don't really understand. Why did it turn out this way? You'd never even seen each other before you met in that beer hall."

"He called me a damned nazi."

"Every policeman gets called a damned nazi several times a week. Hundreds of people have called me a nazi and gestapo man and even worse things, but I've never killed anyone for it."

"He sat there and said it over and over again, damned nazi, damned nazi, damned nazi . . . It was the only thing he said. And he sang."

"Sang?"

"Yes, to get my goat. Annoy me. About Hitler."

"Uh-huh. Well, had you given him any cause to talk like that?"

"I'd told him my old lady was German. That was before."

"Before you began drinking?"

"Yes. Then he just said it didn't matter what kind of mother a guy had."

"And when he was about to go out into the kitchen, you took the bottle and hit him from behind?"

"Yes."

"Did he fall?"

"He sort of fell to his knees. And began bleeding. And then he said, 'You bloody little nazi runt, you, now you're in for it.' "

"And so you went on hitting him?"

"I was . . . afraid. He was bigger than me and . . . you don't know what it feels like . . . everything just goes round and round and goes red . . . I didn't seem to know what I was doing."

The man's shoulders were shaking violently.

"That's enough," said Kollberg, switching off the tape recorder. "Give him something to eat and ask the doctor if he can have a sedative."

The policeman by the door rose, put his cap on and led the murderer out, holding him loosely by the arm.

"Bye for now. See you tomorrow," said Kollberg absently.

At the same time he was writing mechanically on the paper in front of him, "Confessed in tears."

"Quite a character," he said.

"Five previous convictions for assault," said Melander. "In spite of his denying it every time. I remember him very well."

"Said the walking card file," Kollberg commented.

He rose heavily and stared at Martin Beck.

"What are *you* doing here?" he said. "Go take your holiday and let us look after the criminal ways of the lower classes. Where are you going, by the way? To the islands?"

Martin Beck nodded.

"Smart," said Kollberg. "I went to Rumania first and got fried—in Mamaia. Then I come home and get boiled. Great. And you don't have any telephone out there?"

"No."

"Excellent. I'm going to take a shower now anyhow. Come on. Run along now."

Martin Beck thought it over. The suggestion had its advantages. Among other things, he would get away a day earlier. He shrugged his shoulders.

"I'm leaving. Bye, boys. See you in a month."

Most people's holidays were already over and Stockholm's August-hot streets had begun to fill with people who had spent a few rainy July weeks in tents and trailers and country boardinghouses. During the last few days, the subway had once again become crowded, but it was now the middle of the working day and Martin Beck was almost alone in the car. He sat looking at the dusty greenery outside and was glad that his eagerly awaited holiday had at last begun.

His family had already been out in the archipelago for **a** month. This summer they had had the good fortune to rent a cottage from a distant relative of his wife's, a cottage situated all by itself on a little island in the central part of the archipelago. The relative had gone abroad and the cottage was theirs until the children went back to school.

Martin Beck let himself into his empty flat, went straight into the kitchen and took a beer out of the refrigerator. He took a few gulps standing by the sink, then carried the bottle with him into the bedroom. He undressed and walked out onto the balcony in nothing but his shorts. He sat for a while in the sun, his feet on the balcony rail as he finished off the beer. The heat out there was almost intolerable and when the bottle was empty, he got up and went back into the relative cool of the flat.

He looked at his watch. The boat would be leaving in two hours. The island was located in an area of the archipelago where transportation to and from the city was still maintained by one of the few remaining old steamers. This, thought Martin Beck, was just about the best part of their summer holiday find.

He went out into the kitchen and put the empty bottle down on the pantry floor. The pantry had already been cleared of everything that might spoil, but for safety's sake he looked around to see if he had forgotten anything before he shut the pantry door. Then he pulled the refrigerator plug out of the wall, put the ice trays in the sink and looked around the kitchen before shutting the door and going into the bedroom to pack.

Most of what he needed for himself he had already taken out to the island on the weekend he had already spent there. His wife had given him a list of things which she and the children wanted brought out, and by the time he had included everything, he had two bags full. As he also had to pick up a carton of food from the supermarket, he decided to take a taxi to the boat.

There was plenty of room on board and when Martin Beck had put his bags down, he went up on deck and sat down.

The heat was trembling over the city and it was almost dead

calm. The foliage in Karl XII Square had lost its freshness and the flags on the Grand Hotel were drooping. Martin Beck looked at his watch and waited impatiently for the men down there to pull in the gangplank.

When he felt the first vibrations from the engine, he got up and walked to the stern. The boat backed away from the quay and he leaned over the railing, watching the propellers whipping up the water into a whitish-green foam. The steam whistle sounded hoarsely, and as the boat began to turn toward Saltsjön, its hull shuddering, Martin Beck stood by the railing and turned his face toward the cool breeze. He suddenly felt free and untroubled; for a brief moment he seemed to relive the feeling he had had as a boy on the first day of the summer holidays.

He had dinner in the dining saloon, then went out and sat on deck again. Before approaching the jetty where he was to land, the boat passed his island, and he saw the cottage and some gaily colored garden chairs and his wife down on the shore. She was crouching at the water's edge, and he guessed she was scrubbing potatoes. She rose and waved, but he was not certain she could see him at such a distance with the afternoon sun in her eyes.

The children came out to meet him in the rowboat. Martin Beck liked rowing, and ignoring his son's protests, he took the oars and rowed across the bay between the steamer jetty and the island. His daughter—whose name was Ingrid, but who was called Baby although she would be fifteen in a few days—sat in the stern telling about a barn dance. Rolf, who was thirteen and despised girls, was talking about a pike he had landed. Martin listened absently, enjoying the rowing.

After he had taken off his city clothes, he took a brief swim by the rock before pulling on his blue trousers and sweater. After dinner he sat chatting with his wife outside the cottage, watching the sun go down behind the islands on the other side of the mirror-smooth bay. He went to bed early, after setting out some nets with his son.

For the first time in a very long time, he fell asleep immediately.

When he woke, the sun was still low and there was dew on the grass as he padded out and sat down on a rock outside the cottage. It looked as if the day would be as fine as the previous one, but the sun had not yet begun to grow warm, and he was cold in his pajamas. After a while he went in again and sat down on the veranda with a cup of coffee. When it was seven, he dressed and woke his son, who got up reluctantly. They rowed out and hauled in the nets, which contained nothing but a mass of seaweed and water plants. When they got back, the other two were up and breakfast was on the table.

After breakfast Martin Beck went down to the shed and began to hang up and clean the nets. It was work that tried his patience and he decided that in the future he ought to make his son responsible for providing fish for the family.

He had almost finished the last net when he heard the stutter of a motorboat behind him, and a small fishing boat rounded the point, heading straight for him. At once he recognized the man in the boat. It was Nygren, the owner of a small boatyard on the next island, and their nearest neighbor. As there was no water on the Becks' island, they fetched their drinking water from him. Nygren also had a telephone.

Nygren turned off the motor and shouted:

"Telephone. They want you to call back as soon as possible. I wrote the number down on a slip of paper by the telephone."

"Didn't he say who he was?" said Martin Beck, although he in fact already knew.

"I wrote that down too. I've got to go out to Skärholmen now, and Elsa's in the strawberry patch, but the kitchen door's open."

Nygren started up the motor again and, standing in the stern, headed out toward the bay. Before he vanished around the point, he raised his hand in farewell.

Martin Beck watched him for a short while. Then he went down to the jetty, untied the rowboat and began to row toward

Nygren's boathouse. As he rowed he thought: Hell. To hell with Kollberg, just when I'd almost forgotten he existed!

On the pad below the wall telephone in Nygren's kitchen was written, almost illegibly: Hammar 54 10 60.

Martin Beck dialed the number and not until he was waiting for the exchange to put him through did he begin to feel real alarm.

"Hammar speaking," said Hammar.

"Well, what's happened?"

"I'm really sorry, Martin, but I've got to ask you to come in as soon as possible. You may have to sacrifice the rest of your holiday. Well, postpone it, that is."

Hammar was silent for a few seconds. Then he said, "If you will."

"The rest of my holiday? I haven't even had a day of it yet."

"Awfully sorry, Martin, but I wouldn't ask you if it wasn't necessary. Can you get in today?"

"Today? What's happened?"

"If you can get in today, it'd be a good thing. It's really important. I'll tell you more about it when you're here."

"There's a boat in an hour," said Martin Beck, looking out through the fly-specked window at the glittering, sunlit bay. "What's so important about it? Couldn't Kollberg or Melander—"

"No. You'll have to handle this. Someone seems to have disappeared."

When Martin Beck opened the door to his chief's room it was ten to one and he had been on holiday for exactly twenty-four hours.

Chief Inspector Hammar was a heavily built man with a bullneck and bushy gray hair. He sat quite still in his swivel chair, his forearms resting on the top of his desk, completely absorbed in what malicious tongues maintained was his favorite occupation: namely, doing nothing whatsoever.

"Oh, you've arrived," he said sourly. "Just in time too. You're due at the F.O. in half an hour."

"The Foreign Office?"

"Precisely. You're to see this man."

Hammar was holding a calling card by one corner, between his thumb and forefinger, as if it were a piece of lettuce with a caterpillar on it. Martin Beck looked at the name. It meant nothing to him.

"A higher-up," said Hammar. "Considers himself very close to the Minister." He paused slightly, then said, "I've never heard of the fellow either."

Hammar was fifty-nine and had been a policeman since 1927. He did not like politicians.

"You don't look so angry as you ought to," said Hammar.

Martin Beck puzzled on this for a moment. He decided that he was much too confused to be angry.

"What is this actually all about?"

"We'll talk about it later. When you've met this nitwit here."

"You said something about a disappearance."

Hammar stared in torment out through the window, then shrugged his shoulders and said, "The whole thing's quite idiotic. To tell you the truth, I've had . . . instructions not to give you any so-called further information until you've been to the F.O."

"Have we started taking orders from them too?"

"As you know, there are several departments," said Hammar dreamily.

His look became lost somewhere in the summer foliage. He said, "Since I began here we have had a whole regiment of Ministers. The overwhelming majority of them have known just about as much about the police as I know about the orange-shell louse. Namely, that it exists.

"G'bye," he said abruptly.

"Bye," said Martin Beck.

When Martin Beck reached the door, Hammar returned to the present and said, "Martin."

"Yes."

"One thing I can tell you, anyhow. You needn't take this on if you don't want to."

The man who was close to the Minister was large, angular and red-haired. He stared at Martin Beck with watery blue eyes, rose swiftly and expansively and rushed around his desk with his arm outstretched.

"Splendid," he said. "Splendid of you to come."

They shook hands with great enthusiasm. Martin Beck said nothing.

The man returned to his swivel chair, grabbed his cold pipe and bit on the stem of it with his large yellow horse teeth. Then he heaved himself backward in his chair, jammed a thumb into the bowl of his pipe, lit a match and fixed his visitor with a cold, appraising look through the cloud of smoke.

"No ceremony," he said. "I always begin a serious conversation this way. Spit in each other's faces. Things seem to go along more easily afterward. My name's Martin."

"So's mine," said Martin Beck gloomily.

A moment later, he added, "That's unfortunate. Perhaps it complicates the issue."

This seemed to confound the man. He looked sharply at Martin Beck, as if sensing some treachery ahead. Then he laughed uproariously.

"Of course. Funny. Ha ha ha."

Suddenly he fell silent and threw himself at the intercom. Pressing the buttons nervously, he mumbled, "Yes, yes. Really damned funny."

There was not a spark of humor in his voice.

"May I have the Alf Matsson file," he called.

A middle-aged woman came in with a file and put it down on the desk in front of him. He did not even condescend to glance at her. When she had closed the door behind her, he turned his cold, impersonal fisheyes on Martin Beck, slowly opening the file at the same time. It contained one single sheet of paper, covered with scrawled pencil notes.

"This is a tricky and damned unpleasant story," he said.

"Oh," said Martin Beck. "In what way?"

"Do you know Matsson?"

Martin Beck shook his head.

"No? He's quite well known, actually. Journalist. Mainly in the weeklies. Television too. A clever writer. Here."

He opened a drawer and rummaged around in it, then in another, finally lifting up his blotter and finding the object of his search.

"I hate carelessness," he said, throwing a spiteful look in the direction of the door.

Martin Beck studied the object, which turned out to be a neatly typed index card containing certain information about a person by the name of Alf Matsson. The man did indeed appear to be a journalist, employed by one of the larger weeklies, one which Martin Beck himself never read but sometimes saw—with unspoken anxiety and distrust—in the hands of his children. In addition, Alf Sixten Matsson was said to have been born in Gothenburg in 1934. Clipped to the card was also an ordinary passport photograph. Martin Beck cocked his head and looked at a fairly young man with a mustache, a short neat beard and round steel-rimmed glasses. His face was so utterly expressionless that the picture must have come from one of those photo booths around town. Martin Beck put the card down and looked questioningly at the red-haired man.

"Alf Matsson has disappeared," said the man with great emphasis.

"Oh, yes? And your inquiries haven't produced any results?"

"No inquiries have been made. And none are going to be made either," said the man, staring like a maniac.

Martin Beck, who did not realize at first that that watery look testified to a steely determination, frowned slightly.

"How long has he been gone?"

"Ten days."

The reply did not especially surprise him. If the man had said ten minutes or ten years, it would not have moved him particularly either. The only thing that surprised Martin Beck at that moment was the fact that he was sitting here and not in a rowboat out at the island. He looked at his watch. He would probably have time to catch the evening boat back.

"Ten days isn't very long," he said mildly.

Another official came in from a nearby room and entered into the conversation so directly that he must have been listening at the door. Apparently some kind of caretaker, thought Martin Beck.

"In this particular case, it's more than enough," said the new arrival. "The circumstances are highly exceptional. Alf Matsson flew to Budapest on the twenty-second of July, sent there by his magazine to write some articles. On the next Monday, he was to call the office here in Stockholm and read the text of a kind of regular column he writes every week. He didn't. It's relevant that Alf Matsson always delivered on time, as newspaper people say. In other words, he doesn't miss a deadline when it comes to turning in manuscripts. Two days later, the office phoned his hotel in Budapest, where they said that he *was* staying there, but he didn't seem to be in at that moment. The office left a message to say that Matsson should immediately inform Stockholm the moment he came in. They waited for two more days. Nothing was heard. They checked with his wife here in Stockholm. She hadn't heard anything either. That in itself wouldn't necessarily mean anything, as they're getting a divorce. Last Saturday the editor called us up here. By then they had contacted the hotel again and been told that no one there had seen Matsson since they called last, but that his things were still in his room and his passport was still at the reception desk. Last Monday, the first of August, we communicated with our people down there. They knew nothing about Matsson, but put out a feeler, as they called it, to the Hungarian police, who appeared 'not interested.' Last Tuesday we had a visit from the editor in chief of the magazine. It was a very unpleasant meeting."

The redheaded man had definitely been upstaged. He bit on the stem of his pipe in annoyance and said, "Yes, exactly. Damned unpleasant."

A moment later he added by way of explanation: "This is my secretary."

"Well," said his secretary, "anyhow, the result of that conversation was that yesterday we made unofficial contact with the police at top level, which in turn led to your coming here today. Pleased to have you here, by the way."

They shook hands. Martin Beck could not yet see the pattern. He massaged the bridge of his nose thoughtfully.

"I'm afraid I don't really understand," he said. "Why didn't the editors report the matter in the ordinary way?"

"You'll see why in a moment. The editor in chief and responsible publisher of the magazine—the same person, in fact—did not want to report the matter to the police or demand an official investigation because then the case would become known at once and would get into the rest of the press. Matsson is the magazine's own correspondent, and he has disappeared on a reporting trip abroad, so—rightly or wrongly—the magazine regards this as its own news. The editor in chief did seem rather worried about Matsson, but on the other hand, he made no bones about the fact that he smelled a scoop, as they say, news of the caliber that increases a publication's circulation by perhaps a hundred thousand copies just like that. If you know anything about the general line this magazine takes, then you ought to know . . . Well, anyhow, one of its correspondents has disappeared and the fact that he's done it in Hungary, of all places, doesn't make it any worse news."

"Behind the Iron Curtain," said the red-haired man gravely.

"We don't use expressions like that," said the other man. "Well, I hope you realize what all this means. If the case is reported and gets into the papers, that's bad enough—even if

17

the story retained some kind of reasonable proportions and did get a relatively factual treatment. But if the magazine keeps everything to itself and uses it for its own, opinion-leading purpose, then heaven only knows what . . . Well, anyhow it would damage important relations, which both we and other people have spent a long time and a good deal of effort building up. The magazine's editor had a copy of a completed article with him when he was here on Monday. We had the dubious pleasure of reading it. If it's published, it would mean absolute disaster in some respects. And they were actually intending to publish it in this week's issue. We had to use all our powers of persuasion and appeal to every conceivable ethical standard to put a stop to its publication. The whole thing ended with the editor in chief delivering an ultimatum. If Matsson has not made his presence known of his own accord or if we haven't found him before the end of next week . . . well, then sparks are going to fly."

Martin Beck massaged the roots of his hair.

"I suppose the magazine is making its own investigations," he said.

The official looked absently at his superior, who was now puffing away furiously on his pipe.

"I got the impression that the magazine's efforts in that direction were somewhat modest. That their activities in this particular respect had been put on ice until further notice. For that matter, they haven't the slightest idea as to where Matsson is."

"The man does undoubtedly seem to have disappeared," said Martin Beck.

"Yes, exactly. It's very worrisome."

"But he can't have just gone up in smoke," said the red-haired man.

Martin Beck rested one elbow on the edge of the table, clenched his fist and pressed his knuckles against the bridge of his nose. The steamer and the island and the jetty became more and more distant and diffuse in his mind.

"Where do I come into the picture?" he said.

"That was our idea, but naturally we didn't know it would be you personally. We can't investigate all this, least of all in ten days. Whatever's happened, if the man for some reason is keeping under cover, if he's committed suicide, if he's had an accident or . . . something else, then it's a police matter. I mean, insofar as the job can be done only by a professional. So, quite unofficially, we contacted the police at top level. Someone seems to have recommended you. Now it's largely a matter of whether you will take on the case. The fact that you've come here at all indicates that you can be released from your other duties, I suppose."

Martin Beck suppressed a laugh. Both officials looked at him sternly. Presumably they found his behavior inappropriate.

"Yes, I can probably be released," he said, thinking about his nets and the rowboat. "But exactly what do you think I'd be able to do?"

The official shrugged his shoulders.

"Go down there, I suppose. Find him. You can go tomorrow morning if you like. Everything is arranged, by way of our channels. You'll be temporarily transferred to our payroll, but you've no official assignment. Naturally we'll help you in every possible way. For example, if you want to you can make contact with the police down there—or otherwise not. And as I said, you can leave tomorrow."

Martin Beck thought about it.

"The day after tomorrow, in that case."

"That's all right too."

"I'll let you know this afternoon."

"Don't think about it too long, though."

"I'll phone in about an hour. Good-bye."

The red-haired man rushed up and round his desk. He thumped Martin Beck on the back with his left hand and shook hands with his right.

"Well, good-bye then. Good-bye, Martin. And do what you can. This is important."

"It really is," said the other man.

"Yes," said the redhead, "we might have another Wallenberg affair on our hands."

"That was the word we were told not to mention," said the other man in weary despair.

Martin Beck nodded and left.

4

"Are you going out there?" said Hammar.

"Don't know yet. I don't even know the language."

"Neither does anyone else on the force. You can be quite sure we checked. Anyhow, they say you can get by with German and English."

"Odd story."

"Stupid story," said Hammar. "But I know something that those people at the F.O. don't know. We've got a dossier on him."

"Alf Matsson?"

"Yes. The Third Section had it. In the secret files."

"Counter-Espionage?"

"Exactly. The Security Division. An investigation was made on this guy three months ago."

There was a deafening thumping on the door and Kollberg thrust his head in. He stared at Martin Beck in astonishment.

"What are you doing here?"

"Having my holiday."

"What's all this hush-hush you're up to? Shall I go away? As quietly as I came, without anybody noticing?"

"Yes," said Hammar. "No, don't. I'm tired of hush-hush. Come in and shut the door."

He pulled a file out of a desk drawer.

"This was a routine investigation," he said, "and it gave rise to no particular action. But parts of it might interest anyone who is thinking of looking into the case."

"What the hell are you up to?" said Kollberg. "Have you opened a secret agency or something?"

"If you don't pipe down, you can go," said Martin Beck. "Why was Counter-Espionage interested in Matsson?"

"The passport people have their own little eccentricities. At Arlanda airport, for instance, they write down the names of people who travel to those European countries that require visas. Some bright boy who looked in their books got it into his head that this Matsson traveled all too often. To Warsaw, Prague, Budapest, Sofia, Bucharest, Constanta, Belgrade. He was great for using his passport."

"And?"

"So Security did a little hush-hush investigation. They went, for instance, to the magazine he works for and asked."

"And what did they reply?"

"Perfectly correct, said the magazine. Alf Matsson *is* a great one for using his passport. Why shouldn't he be? He's our expert on Eastern European affairs. The results are no more remarkable than that. But there are one or two things. Take this rubbish and read it for yourself. You can sit here. Because now I'm going to go home. And this evening I'm going to go to a James Bond film. Bye!"

Martin Beck picked up the report and began to read. When he had finished the first page, he pushed it over to Kollberg, who picked it up between the tips of his fingers and placed it down in front of him. Martin Beck looked questioningly at him.

"I sweat so much," said Kollberg. "Don't want to mess up their secret documents."

Martin Beck nodded. He himself never sweated except when he had a cold.

They said nothing for the following half hour.

The dossier did not offer much of immediate interest, but it was very thoroughly compiled. Alf Matsson was not born in

Gothenburg in 1934, but in Mölndal in 1933. He had begun as a journalist in the provinces in 1952 and been a reporter on several daily papers before going to Stockholm as a sports writer in 1955. As a sports reporter, he had made several trips abroad, among others to the Olympic Games, in Melbourne in 1956 and in Rome in 1960. A number of editors vouchsafed that he was a skillful journalist: ". . . adroit, with a speedy pen." He had left the daily press in 1961, when he was taken on by the weekly for which he still worked. During the last four years he had devoted more and more of his time to overseas reporting on a very wide variety of subjects, from politics and economics to sport and pop stars. He had taken his university entrance exam and spoke fluent English and German, passable Spanish and some French and Russian. He earned over 40,000 kronor a year and had been married twice. His first marriage took place in 1954 and was dissolved the following year. He had married again in 1961 and had two children, a daughter by his first marriage and a son by his second.

With praiseworthy diligence, the investigator now went over to the man's less admirable points. On several occasions he had neglected to pay maintenance for his elder child. His first wife described him as a "drunkard and a brutal beast." Parenthetically, it was pointed out that this witness appeared to be not entirely reliable. There were, however, several indications that Alf Matsson drank, among others a remark in a statement by an ex-colleague who said that he was "all right, but a bastard when he got drunk," but only one of these statements was supported by evidence. On the eve of Twelfth Day in 1966, a radio patrol in Malmö had taken him to the emergency room of General Hospital after he had been stabbed in the hand during a brawl at the home of a certain Bengt Jönsson, whom he had happened to be visiting. The case was investigated by the police but was not taken to court, as Matsson had not wished to press a charge. However, two policemen by the names of Kristiansson and Kvant described both Matsson and Jönsson as under the influence, so the case was registered at the Commission on Alcoholism.

The tone of the statement by his present boss, an editor called Eriksson, was snooty. Matsson was the magazine's "expert on Eastern Europe" (whatever use a publication of this kind could possibly have for such a person) and the editorial board found no cause to give the police any further information about his journalistic activities. Matsson was, they went on to say, very interested in and well-informed on Eastern European matters, often produced projects of his own, and had on several occasions proved himself ambitious by giving up holidays and days off without extra pay to be able to carry out certain reporting assignments that especially interested him.

Some previous reader had in turn appeared ambitious by underlining this sentence in red. It could hardly have been Hammar, who did not mess up other people's reports.

A detailed account of Matsson's published articles showed that they consisted almost exclusively of interviews with famous athletes and reportage on sports, film stars and other figures from the entertainment world.

The dossier contained several items in the same style. When he had finished reading, Kollberg said, "Singularly uninteresting person."

"There's one peculiar detail."

"That he's disappeared, you mean?"

"Exactly," said Martin Beck.

A minute later, he dialed the Foreign Office number and Kollberg, much to his surprise, heard him say, "'Is that Martin? Yes, hi Martin—this is Martin."

Martin Beck seemed to listen for a moment, a tortured expression on his face. Then he said, "Yes, I'm going."

5

The building was old and had no elevator. Matsson was the top name on the list of tenants down in the entrance hall. When Martin Beck had climbed the five steep flights of stairs, he was out of breath and his heart was thumping. He waited for a moment before ringing the doorbell.

The woman who opened the door was small and fair. She was wearing slacks and a cotton-knit top and had hard lines around her mouth. Martin Beck guessed she was about thirty.

"Come in," she said, holding open the door.

He recognized her voice from the telephone conversation they had had an hour earlier.

The hall of the flat was large and unfurnished except for an unpainted stool along one wall. A small boy of about two or three came out of the kitchen. He had a half-eaten roll in his hand and went straight up to Martin Beck, stood in front of him and stretched up a sticky fist.

"Hi," he said.

Then he turned around and ran into the living room. The woman followed him and lifted up the boy, who with a satisfied gurgle had sat down in the room's only comfortable armchair. The boy yelled as she carried him into a neighboring room and closed the door. She came back, sat down on the sofa and lit a cigarette.

"You want to ask me about Alf. Has something happened to him?"

After a moment's hesitation, Martin Beck sat down on the armchair.

"Not so far as we know. It's just that he doesn't seem to have been heard from for a couple of weeks. Neither by the magazine, nor, so far as I can make out, by you, either. You don't know where he might be?"

"No idea. And the fact that he's not let me know anything isn't very strange in itself. He's not been here for four weeks, and before that I didn't hear from him for a month."

Martin Beck looked toward the closed door.

"But the boy? Doesn't he usually . . ."

"He hasn't seemed especially interested in his son since we've separated," she said, with some bitterness. "He sends money to us every month. But that's only right, don't you think?"

"Does he earn a lot on the magazine?"

"Yes. I don't know how much, but he always had plenty of money. And he wasn't mean. I never had to go without, although he spent a lot of money on himself. In restaurants and on taxis and so on. Now I've got a job, so I earn a little myself."

"How long have you been divorced?"

"We're not divorced. It's not been granted yet. But he moved out of here almost eight months ago now. He got hold of a flat then. But even before that, he was away from home so much that it hardly made any difference."

"But I suppose you're familiar with his habits—who he sees and where he usually goes?"

"Not any longer. To be quite frank, I don't know what he's up to. Before, he used to hang around mostly with people from work. Journalists and the like. They used to sit around in a restaurant called the Tankard. But I don't know now. Maybe he's found some other place. Anyhow, that restaurant's moved or has been torn down, hasn't it?"

She put out her cigarette and went over to the door to listen. Then she opened it cautiously and went in. A moment later she came out and shut the door just as carefully behind her.

"He's asleep," she said.

"Nice little boy," said Martin Beck.

25

"Yes, he's nice."

They sat silent for a moment, and then she said, "But Alf was on an assignment in Budapest, wasn't he? At least, I heard that somewhere. Mightn't he have stayed there? Or have gone somewhere else?"

"Did he used to do that? When he was away on assignments?"

"No," she said hesitantly. "No, actually he didn't. He's not especially conscientious and he drinks a lot, but while we were together he certainly didn't neglect his work. For instance, he was awfully particular about getting his manuscripts in at the time he'd promised. When he lived here, he often sat up late at night writing to get things finished in time."

She looked at Martin Beck. For the first time during their conversation he noticed a vague anxiety in her eyes.

"It does seem peculiar, doesn't it? That he's never got in touch with the magazine. Supposing something really has happened to him."

"Have you any idea what might have happened to him?"

She shook her head.

"No, none at all."

"You said before that he drinks. Does he drink a lot?"

"Yes—sometimes, at least. Toward the end, when he lived here, he often came home drunk. If he generally ever came home at all."

The bitter lines around her mouth had returned.

"But didn't that affect his work?"

"No, it didn't really. Anyhow not much. When he began working for this weekly magazine, he often got special assignments. Abroad and that kind of thing. In between, he didn't have much to do and was often free. He didn't have to be at the office much. That was when he drank. Sometimes he sat around that café for days on end."

"I see," said Martin Beck. "Can you give me the names of anyone he used to go around with?"

She gave Martin Beck the names of three journalists who

were unknown to him, and he wrote them down on a taxi receipt he found in his inside pocket. She looked at him and said:

"I thought the police always had little notebooks with black covers that they wrote everything down in. But maybe that's just in books and at the movies."

Martin Beck got up.

"If you hear anything from him, perhaps you'd be good enough to call me," she said. "Would you?"

"Naturally," said Martin Beck.

In the hall, he asked, "Where did you say he was living now?"

"On Fleminggatan. Number 34. But I didn't say."

"Have you got a key to the apartment?"

"Oh, no. I haven't even been there."

On the door was a piece of cardboard with MATSSON lettered on it in India ink. The lock was an ordinary one and caused Martin Beck no difficulties. Aware that he was over-stepping his authority, he made his way into the flat. On the doormat was some mail—a few advertisements, a postcard from Madrid signed by someone called Bibban, a sports car magazine in English and an electricity bill amounting to 28:45 kronor.

The flat consisted of two large rooms, a kitchen, hall and toilet. There was no washroom, but two large wardrobes. The air in the flat was heavy and musty.

In the largest room, facing the street, were a bed, a night table, bookshelves, a low circular table with a glass top, a desk and two chairs. On the night table stood a record player and on the shelf below, a pile of long-playing records. Martin Beck read in English on the top sleeve: *Blue Monk*. It meant nothing to him. On the desk were a sheaf of typing paper, a daily paper dated July twentieth, a taxi receipt for 6:50 kronor dated the eighteenth, a German dictionary, a magnifying glass and a stenciled information sheet from a youth club. There was a telephone too, and telephone directories and two ash trays. The drawers contained old magazines, magazine photographs, receipts, a few letters and postcards, and a number of carbon copies of manuscripts.

In the back room there was no furniture at all except a narrow divan with a faded red cover, a chair and a stool that served as a night table. There were no curtains.

Martin Beck opened the doors of both wardrobes. One of them contained an almost empty laundry bag and on the shelves lay shirts, sweaters and underclothes, some of them with the laundry's paper bands still unbroken around them. In the other hung two tweed jackets, a dark-brown flannel suit, three pairs of trousers and a winter overcoat. Three hangers were empty. On the floor stood a pair of heavy brown shoes with rubber soles, a pair of thinner black ones, a pair of boots and a pair of galoshes. There was a large suitcase in the cupboard above the one wardrobe, but the other cupboard was empty.

Martin Beck went out into the kitchen. There were no dirty dishes in the sink, but on the drainboard were two glasses and a mug. The pantry was empty except for a few empty wine bottles and two cans. Martin Beck thought about his own pantry, which he had quite unnecessarily cleaned out so thoroughly.

He walked through the flat one more time. The bed was made, the ash trays were empty, and there were neither passport, money, bankbooks nor anything else of value in the drawers of the desk. All in all, there was nothing to indicate that Alf Matsson had been home since he had left the flat and gone to Budapest two weeks previously.

Martin Beck left Alf Matsson's flat and stood for a moment by the deserted taxi stand down on Fleminggatan, but as usual at lunch time there were no taxis available and he took a trolley instead.

It was past one when he went into the dining room of the Tankard. All the tables were taken and the harassed waitresses took no notice of him. There was no headwaiter to be seen. He crossed over to the bar on the other side of the entrance hall. At that moment a fat man in a corduroy jacket gathered up his papers and rose from a round table in the corner next to the door. Martin Beck took his place. Here too, all the tables were full, but some of the customers were just paying their bills.

He ordered a sandwich and beer from the headwaiter and asked if any of the three journalists was there.

"Mr. Molin is sitting over there, but I haven't seen the others today. They'll probably be in later."

Martin Beck followed the headwaiter's glance toward a table where five men were sitting talking with large steins of beer in front of them.

"Which of the gentlemen is Mr. Molin?"

"The gentleman with the beard," said the headwaiter, and went away.

Confused, Martin Beck looked at the five men. Three of them had beards.

The waitress came with his sandwich and beer and gave him the chance to say, "Do you happen to know which of the gentlemen over there is Mr. Molin?"

"Of course, the one with the beard."

She followed his somewhat desperate look and added, "Nearest the window."

Martin Beck ate his sandwich very slowly. The man named Molin ordered another stein of beer. Martin Beck waited. The place began to empty. After a while Molin emptied his stein and was given another. Martin Beck finished eating his sandwich, ordered coffee, and waited.

Finally the man with the beard got up from his place by the window and walked toward the entrance hall. Just as he was passing, Martin Beck said, "Mr. Molin?"

The man stopped. "Just a moment," he said, and went on out.

A short while later, he returned, breathed heavily all over Martin Beck, and said, "Do we know each other?"

"No, not yet. But perhaps you'd like to sit down a moment and have a beer with me. There's something I'd like to ask you about."

He himself could hear that it didn't sound especially good. Smelled of police business a mile away. But it worked anyhow. Molin sat down. He had fair, rather thin hair, combed forward onto his forehead. His beard was reddish and neat. He looked about thirty-five and was quite plump. He waved a waitress over to him.

"Say Stina, get me a round, will you?"

The waitress nodded and looked at Martin Beck.

"The same," he said.

A "round" turned out to be a bulbous and considerably larger stein than the cylindrical though quite large one he himself had drunk with his sandwich.

Molin took a large gulp and wiped his mustache with his handkerchief.

"Uh-huh," he said. "What was it you wanted to talk to me about? Hangovers?"

"About Alf Matsson," said Martin Beck. "You're good friends, aren't you?"

It still didn't sound quite right and he tried to improve on it by saying, "Buddies, aren't you?"

"Of course. What's up with him? Does he owe you money?"

Molin looked suspiciously and haughtily at Martin Beck.

"Well then, I'd first like to point out that I'm not any kind of collection agency."

Clearly, he would have to watch his tongue. Moreover, the man was a journalist.

"No, nothing like that at all," said Martin Beck.

"Then what do you want Alfie for?"

"Alfie and I've known each other for a long time. We

worked on the same . . . well, we were on the same job together a number of years ago. I met him quite by chance a
few weeks ago and he promised to do a job for me, and then I
never heard another word from him. He talked about you quite
a bit, so I thought perhaps you'd know where he was."

Somewhat exhausted by this strenuous oratorical effort,
Martin Beck took a deep gulp of his beer. The other man
followed suit.

"Oh, hell. You're an old pal of Alfie's, are you? The fact is
that I've been wondering where he was too. But I suppose
he's stayed on in Hungary. He's not in town, anyhow. Or we'd
have seen him here."

"In Hungary? What's he doing there?"

"On some trip for that gossip sheet he works for. But he
should really be home by now. When he left, he said he was
only going to be away for two or three days."

"Did you see him before he left?"

"Yes indeed. The night before. We were here in the daytime
and then went to a couple of other places in the evening."

"You and him?"

"Yes, and some of the others. I don't really remember who.
Per Kronkvist and Stig Lund were there, I think. We got
really stoned. Yes, Åke and Pia were there too. Don't you know
Åke, by the way?"

Martin Beck thought. It seemed somewhat pointless.

"Åke? I don't know. Which Åke?"

"Åke Gunnarsson," said Molin, turning around toward the
table where he had been sitting before. Two of the men had
left during their conversation. The two remaining were sitting
silently over their beers.

"He's sitting over there," said Molin. "The guy with the
beard."

One of the beards had gone, so there was no doubt which
of them was Gunnarsson. The man looked quite pleasant.

"No," said Martin Beck. "I don't think I know him. Where
does he work?"

Molin gave the name of a publication that Martin Beck had never heard of, but it sounded like some kind of auto magazine.

"Åke's all right. He got pretty high that night too, if I remember rightly. Otherwise, he doesn't get really drunk very often. No matter how much he pours into himself."

"Haven't you seen Alfie since then?"

"That's a hell of a lot of questions you're asking. Aren't you going to ask me how I am too?"

"Of course. How are you?"

"Absolutely god-damned awful. Hangover. Damned bad one, too."

Molin's fat face grew gloomy. As if to obliterate the last shreds of the pleasures of living, he drank the remains of his beer in one huge gulp. He took out his handkerchief, and with a brooding look in his eyes, mopped his foamy mustache.

"They ought to serve beer in mustache cups," he said. "There isn't much service left these days."

After a brief pause he said, "No, I haven't seen Alfie since he left. The last I saw of him was when he was pouring his drink over some gal in the Opera House bar. Then he went to Budapest the next morning. Poor devil, having to sit up flying right across half of Europe with a hangover like that. Hope he didn't fly Scandinavian Airlines anyhow."

"And you've not heard anything from him since then?"

"We don't usually write letters when we're on overseas trips," said Molin haughtily. "What the hell kind of a rag do you work for, anyhow? The *Kiddy Krib*? Well, what about another round?"

Half an hour and two more rounds later, Martin Beck managed to escape from Mr. Molin, after having first lent him ten kronor. As he left, he heard the man's voice behind him, "Fia, old thing, get me a round, will you?"

7

The plane was an Ilyushin 18 turboprop from Czechoslovak Airlines. It rose in a steep arc over Copenhagen and Saltholm, and an Öresund that glittered in the sun.

Martin Beck sat by the window and looked down at Ven Island below, with Backafall Cliffs, the church and the little harbor. He had just had time to see a tugboat rounding the harbor pier before the plane turned south.

He liked traveling, but this time disappointment over his spoiled holiday overshadowed most of his pleasure. Moreover, his wife had not seemed to understand at all that his own choice in the matter had not been very great. He had called the evening before and tried to explain, but had not been particularly successful.

"You don't care a bit about me or the children," she had said.

And a moment later:

"There must be *other* policemen besides you. Do you have to take on *every* assignment?"

He had tried to convince her that he would in fact have preferred to go out to the island, but she had gone on being unreasonable. In addition, she had demonstrated various evidence of faulty logic.

"So you're going to Budapest to enjoy yourself while the children and I are stuck by ourselves out on this island."

"I am not going for fun."

"Hmm-mph."

In the end she had put down the receiver in the middle of a sentence. He knew she would calm down eventually, but he had not attempted to call again.

Now, at an altitude of 16,000 feet, he tipped his seat back, lit a cigarette and let his thoughts of the island and his family sink into the back of his mind.

During their stopover at Schönefeld airport in East Berlin, he drank a beer in the transit lounge. He noted that the beer was called Radeberger. It was excellent beer, but he didn't think he would have cause to remember the name. The waiter entertained him in Berlin German. He did not understand very much of it and wondered gloomily how he was going to manage in the future.

In a basket by the entrance lay a few pamphlets in German and he took one out at random to have something to read while he waited. Clearly he needed to practice his German.

The leaflet was published by the German journalist's union and dealt with the Springer concern, one of the most powerful newspaper and magazine publishers in West Germany, and its chief, Axel Springer. It gave examples of the company's menacing fascist politics and quoted several of its more prominent contributors.

When his flight was called, Martin Beck noted that he had read almost the whole pamphlet without difficulty. He put the pamphlet into his pocket and boarded the plane.

After an hour in the air, the plane again came down to land, this time in Prague, a city that Martin Beck had always wanted to visit. Now he had to be content with a brief glimpse, from the air, of its many towers and bridges and of the Moldau; the stopover was too short to give him time to get into the city from the airport.

His red-haired namesake in the Foreign Office had apologized for the connections between Stockholm and Budapest which were not the world's best, but Martin Beck had no objections to the delays, although he was not able to see more of Berlin and Prague than their transit lounges.

Martin Beck had never been to Budapest and when the

plane had taken off again, he read through a couple of leaflets
he had received from the redhead's secretary. In one dealing
with the geography of Hungary, he read that Budapest had two
million inhabitants. He wondered how he was going to find
Alf Matsson if the man had decided to disappear in this
metropolis.

In his mind he reviewed what he knew about Alf Matsson.
It was not a great deal, but he wondered whether there was
really anything else to know. He thought of Kollberg's comment: "Singularly uninteresting person." Why should a man
like Alf Matsson want to disappear? That is, if he had disappeared of his own free will? A woman? It seemed hardly credi-
ble that he should sacrifice a well-paid position—one that
he seemed to be happy with, moreover—for that reason. He was
still married, of course, but perfectly free to do as he wished.
He had a home, work, money and friends. It was hard to think
of any plausible reason why he should voluntarily leave all that.

Martin Beck took out the copy of the personal file from the
Security Division. Alf Matsson had become an object of interest
to the police simply because of his many and frequent trips to
places in Eastern Europe. "Behind the Iron Curtain," the redhead had said. Well, the man was a reporter, and if he preferred
to undertake assignments in Eastern Europe, then that in itself
wasn't so peculiar. And if he had anything on his conscience
now, why should he disappear? The Security Division had con-
signed the case to oblivion after a routine investigation. "A
new Wallenberg affair," the man at the F.O. had said, thinking of the famous case of a well-known Swede last seen in
Budapest in 1945: "Spirited away by the Communists." "You
see too many James Bond movies," Kollberg would have said
if he had been there.

Martin Beck folded up the copy and put it into his briefcase. He looked out the window. It was completely dark now
but the stars were out, and way down there he could see small
dots of light from villages and communities and pearl strings
of light where the street lamps were on.

Perhaps Matsson had started to drink, abandoning the magazine and everything else. When he sobered up again he would be broke and full of remorse and would have to make his presence known. But that didn't sound likely either. True, he drank occasionally, but not to that degree, and normally he never neglected his job.

Perhaps he had committed suicide, had an accident, fallen into the Danube and drowned or been robbed and killed. Was this more likely? Hardly. Somewhere or other, Martin Beck had read that, of all the capitals in the world, Budapest had the lowest crime rate.

Perhaps he was sitting in the hotel dining room right now, having his dinner, and Martin Beck would be able to take the plane back the next day and continue his holiday.

The signs lit up. No smoking. Please fasten your seatbelts. And then they repeated the same thing in Russian.

When the plane stopped taxiing, Martin Beck picked up his briefcase and walked the short stretch toward the airport buildings. The air was soft and warm although it was late in the evening.

He had to wait quite a long time for his only suitcase, but the passport and customs formalities were dispensed with swiftly. He went through a huge lounge, its walls lined with shops, and then out onto the steps outside the building. The airport appeared to be far outside the city. He saw no other lights except those within the area of the airport itself. As he stood there, two elderly ladies climbed into the only taxi there was on the turn-around drive in front of the steps.

Some time elapsed before the next taxi drove up, and as it took him through suburbs and dark industrial areas, Martin Beck realized he was hungry. He knew nothing about the hotel he was going to stay at—other than its name and the fact that Alf Matsson had stayed there before he had disappeared—but he hoped he would be able to get something to eat there.

The taxi drove along broad streets and around large open squares into what appeared to be the center of the city. There were not many people about and most of the streets were empty and rather dark. For a while they went down a wide street with brightly lit store windows before continuing into narrower and darker side streets. Martin Beck had no idea whatsoever where he was in the city, but all the while he kept an eye out for the river.

The taxi stopped outside the lighted entrance of the hotel. Martin Beck leaned over and read the figure on the red meter before paying the driver. It seemed expensive, more than a hundred forints. He had forgotten what a forint was worth in his own money, but he realized that it couldn't be very much.

An elderly man, with a gray mustache, a green uniform and visored cap, opened the taxi door and took his bag. Martin Beck walked through the revolving doors behind him. The entrance hall was large and very lofty, the reception desk running at an angle across the left-hand corner of the hall. The night porter spoke English. Martin Beck gave him his passport and asked if he could have dinner. The porter indicated a glass door farther down the hall and explained that the dining room was open until midnight. Then he gave the key to the waiting elevator man who took Martin Beck's bag and preceded him into the elevator. The car creaked its way up to the first floor. The elevator man appeared to be at least as old as the elevator, and Martin Beck tried in vain to relieve him of the bag. They walked down a long corridor, turned to the left twice, and then the old man unlocked some enormous double doors and put the bag inside.

The room was over twelve feet high and very large. The mahogany furniture was dark and huge. Martin Beck opened the door to the bathroom. The bathtub was spacious with large, old-fashioned taps and a shower.

The windows were high and had shutters on the inside, and in front of the window alcove hung heavy white lace curtains. He opened the shutters on one side and looked out. Immediately below was a gas lamp, throwing out a yellowish-green light. Far away he could see lights, but quite a time elapsed before he realized that the river was flowing between him and the lights over there.

He opened the window and leaned out. Below, a stone

balustrade and large flower urns encompassed tables and chairs. Light was streaming out onto them, and he could hear a little orchestra playing a Strauss waltz. Between the hotel and the river ran a road with trees and gas lamps, a trolley line and a broad quay, on which there were benches and big flower pots. Two bridges, one to his right and the other to the left, spanned the river.

He left the window open and went down to eat. Opening the glass doors from the hall, he came into a lobby with deep armchairs, low tables and mirrors along one wall. Two steps led up to the dining room and at the far end sat the little orchestra he had heard up in his room.

The dining room was colossal, with two huge mahogany pillars and a balcony running along three of the walls, high up under the roof. Three waiters wearing reddish-brown jackets with black lapels were standing inside the door. They bowed and greeted him in chorus, while a fourth rushed forward and directed him to a table near the window and the orchestra.

Martin Beck stared at the menu for a long time before he found the column written in German and began to read. After a while the waiter, a gray-haired man with the physiognomy of a friendly boxer, leaned over toward him and said:

"Very gut Fischsuppe, gentleman."

Martin Beck at once decided upon fish soup.

"*Barack?*" said the waiter.

"What's that?" said Martin Beck, first in German, then in English.

"Very gut apéritif," said the waiter.

Martin Beck drank the apéritif called *barack. Barack palinka,* explained the waiter, was Hungarian apricot brandy.

He ate the fish soup, which was red and strongly spiced with paprika and was indeed very good.

He ate fillet of veal with potatoes in strong paprika sauce and he drank Czechoslovakian beer.

When he had finished his coffee, which was strong, and an additional *barack,* he felt very sleepy and went straight up to his room.

He shut the window and the shutters and crept into bed. It creaked. It creaked in a friendly way, he thought, and fell asleep.

8

Martin Beck was waked by a hoarse, long-drawn-out toot. As he tried to orient himself, blinking in the half-light, the toot was repeated twice. He turned over on his side and picked his wristwatch up off the night table. It was already ten to nine. The great bed creaked ceremoniously. Perhaps, he thought, it had once creaked as majestically beneath Field Marshal Conrad von Hötzendorf. The daylight was trickling through the shutters. It was already very warm in the room.

He got up, went out into the bathroom and coughed for a while, as he usually did in the mornings. After drinking a gulp of mineral water, he pulled on his dressing gown and opened the shutters and the window. The contrast between the dusky light of the room and the clear, sharp sunlight outside was almost overwhelming. So was the view.

The Danube was flowing past him on its calm, even course from north to south, not especially blue, but wide and majestic and indubitably very beautiful. On the other side of the river rose two softly curved hills crowned by a monument and a walled fortress. Houses clambered only hesitantly along the sides of the hills, but farther away were other hills strewn with villas. That was the famous Buda side, then, and there you were very close to the heart of central European culture. Martin Beck let his glance roam over the panoramic view, absently listening to the wingbeats of history. There the Romans had founded their mighty settlement Aquincum, from there the Hapsburg artillery had shot Pest into ruins during the War of Liberation of 1849, and there Szalasis' fascists and Lieutenant General Pfeffer-Wildenbruch's SS troops had stayed for a whole month during the spring of 1945, with a meaningless heroism that invited annihilation (old fascists he had met in Sweden still spoke of it with pride).

Immediately below lay a white paddle steamer tied up to the quay, with its red, white and blue Czechoslovak flag hanging limply in the heat and tourists sunbathing in deckchairs on board. What had waked him was a Yugoslavian paddle-wheel tugboat that was slowly struggling upstream. It was big and old, with two tall funnels tilting asymmetrically, and it was pulling six heavily loaded barges. On the last barge a line had been strung between the wheelhouse and the low loading crane between the hatches. A young woman in a head scarf and blue work garb was tranquilly picking washing out of a basket and carefully hanging up baby clothes, unmoved by the beauty of the shores. To the left, arching over the river, was a long, airy, slender bridge. It seemed to lead directly to the mountain with the monument—a tall, slim bronze woman with a palm leaf raised above her head. Across the bridge thronged cars, buses, trolleys and pedestrians. To the right, northward, the tugboat had reached the next bridge. Again it let out three hoarse toots to announce the number of barges it was pulling, let down its funnels fore and aft and slid in under the low arch of the bridge. Just in front of the window a very small steamer swung in toward the shore, slid over fifty yards athwartship with the current and smartly completed the maneuver, putting in with hardly an inch to spare at a pontoon jetty. A preposterous number of people went ashore from the steamer and an equally preposterous number then boarded it.

The air was dry and warm. The sun was high. Martin Beck leaned out of the window, letting his eyes sweep from north to south as he considered a few facts he had gleaned from the brochures he had read on the plane.

"Budapest is the capital of the Hungarian People's Republic. It is considered to have been founded in 1873, when the three towns Buda, Pest and Óbuda were united into one, but excavations have revealed settlements several thousand years old, and

Aquincum, the capital of the Roman province of Lower Pannonia, was situated on this spot. Today the city has nearly two million inhabitants and is divided into twenty-three districts."

It was certainly a very large city. He remembered the legendary Gustaf Lidberg's almost classic reflection on landing in New York in 1899, on his search for the counterfeiter Skog: "In this ant-heap is Mr. Who, address: Where?"

Well, New York was certainly larger than this, even at that time, but on the other hand, Chief Detective Lidberg had had unlimited time at his disposal. He himself had only a week.

Martin Beck left history and the river traffic to their respective fates and went and took a shower. He put on his sandals and his light-gray Dacron slacks and wore his shirt outside. As he critically observed his unconventional attire in the mirror in the huge wardrobe, the mahogany doors suddenly opened by themselves, slowly and fatefully, with an unnerving creak, as in early thriller films. He still hadn't got his pulse under control when the telephone began to ring with short, urgent little signals.

"There's a gentleman to see you. He's waiting in the foyer. A Swedish gentleman."

"Is it Mr. Matsson?"

"Yes, I'm sure it is," said the receptionist happily.

Of course it is, thought Martin Beck as he went down the stairs. In that case there would be a thoroughly honorable end to this odd assignment.

It was not Alf Matsson, but a young man from the Embassy, extremely correctly dressed in a dark suit, black shoes, white shirt and a pale-gray silk tie. The man's eyes ran over Martin Beck, a glint of wonder in them, but only a glint.

"As you will understand, we are aware of the nature of your assignment. Perhaps we should discuss the matter."

They sat down in the lobby and discussed the matter.

"There are better hotels than this one," said the man from the Embassy.

"Really?"

"Yes. More modern. Tip-top. Swimming pool."

"Oh yes."

"The night club here isn't much good either."

"Oh yes."

"With regard to this Alf Matsson."

The man lowered his voice and looked around the lobby, which was empty except for an African sleeping in the farthest corner.

"Yes. Have you heard from him?"

"No. Nothing at all. The only thing we know for certain is that he checked in at Ferihegyi, that's the airport here, on the evening of the twenty-second. He spent the night at some kind of youth hotel called Ifjuság up on the Buda side. The next morning he moved in here. About half an hour later, he went out and took his room key with him. Since then, no one has seen him."

"What do the police say?"

"Nothing."

"Nothing?"

"The ones I've spoken with don't seem interested. Officially speaking, that attitude is defensible. Matsson had a valid visa and he has registered as a resident at this hotel. The police have no reason to concern themselves with him until he leaves the country, so long as he doesn't overstay the period of his residence permit."

"Couldn't he have left the country?"

"Quite unthinkable. And even if he had succeeded in getting over the border illegally, where would he go then? Without a passport. Anyhow, we've made some inquiries at the embassies in Prague, Belgrade, Bucharest and Vienna. Even in Moscow, for safety's sake. No one knows anything."

"His employer seemed to think that he had two things to do here. An interview with Laszlo Papp, the boxer, and an article on the Jewish museum."

"He hasn't been to either place. We've done a little investigating. He had written a letter from Sweden to the curator of the museum, a Dr. Sos, but did not look him up. We've also talked to Papp's mother. She had never heard of Matsson's name and Papp himself is not even in town."

"Is his luggage still in his hotel room?"

"His possessions are at the hotel. Not in his room. He had reserved a room for three nights only. The hotel management retained it at our request, then moved his luggage into the office. Out here. Behind the reception desk. In fact, it wasn't even unpacked. We paid the bill."

The man sat in silence for a while, as if he were thinking something over. Then he said solemnly, "Naturally we're going to demand the amount back from his employers."

"Or his estate," said Martin Beck.

"Yes, if things turn out to be as bad as that."

"Where's his passport?"

"I have it here," said the man from the Embassy.

He unzipped his flat briefcase, took out the passport and handed it over, simultaneously taking his fountain pen out of his inside pocket.

"Here you are. Would you sign for it, please?"

Martin Beck signed. The man put away his pen and the receipt.

"Well, then. Is there anything else? Yes, of course, the hotel bill. You needn't worry about that. We've had instructions to cover your expenses. Rather unorthodox, I feel. Naturally you should have had daily expenses in the usual fashion. Well, if you need any cash, you can collect it at the Embassy."

"Thank you."

"Then I don't think there's anything else, is there? You can go through his possessions whenever you like. I've let them know."

The man got up.

"In fact you're occupying the same room that Matsson had," he said in passing. "It's 105, isn't it? If we hadn't insisted on the room remaining in Matsson's name, you would probably have had to stay at some other hotel. It's the height of the season."

Before they parted, Martin Beck said, "What do you personally think about this? Where's he gone?"

The man from the Embassy looked at him expressionlessly. "If I think anything at all, I prefer to keep it to myself."

A moment later he added, "This thing is very unpleasant."

Martin Beck went up to his room. It had already been cleaned. He looked around. So Alf Matsson had stayed here, had he? For an hour, at the most. To expect any clues from his activities during that brief period would be demanding too much.

What had Alf Matsson done during that hour? Had he stood by the window like this, looking out at the boats? Perhaps. Had he seen somebody or something that made him leave the hotel so quickly he'd forgotten to hand in his key? Possibly. What would it have been, then? Impossible to say. If he'd been run over in the street, it would have been reported at once. If he had planned to jump into the river, he would have had to wait until dark. If he had tried to nurse his hangover with apricot brandy and had plunged into another drinking bout as a result, then he'd had sixteen days in which to sober up. That was a bit much. Anyway, he had not been in the habit of drinking while on an assignment. He was the modern type of journalist, it had said someplace in the report from the Third Division: quick, efficient and direct. He was the type who did the job first and relaxed afterward.

Unpleasant. Very unpleasant. Singularly unpleasant. Damned unpleasant. Blasted unpleasant. Almost painfully so.

Martin Beck lay down on the bed. It creaked magnificently. Gone were thoughts of Baron Conrad von Hötzendorf. Had it scrunched beneath Alf Matsson? Presumably. Was there anybody who didn't test the bed as soon as he stepped into a hotel room? So Matsson had lain here and looked up at the ceiling over twelve feet above. Then, without unpacking and without handing in his key, he had gone out . . . and disappeared. Had the telephone rung? With some startling news?

Martin Beck unfolded his map of Budapest and studied it at

length. Then he was seized with an urge to perform some kind of duty, so he rose, put the map and his passport into his hip pocket and went down to inspect the luggage.

The porter was a somewhat stout, elderly man, friendly, dignified and admirably intelligible.

No, no one had phoned Mr. Matsson while Mr. Matsson was still in the hotel. Later, when Mr. Matsson had left, there had been several calls. They had been repeated the following days. Was it the same person who had phoned? No, several different people—the operator at the board was sure of that. Men? Both men and women, at least one woman. Had the people who had phoned left any messages or telephone numbers? No, they had left no messages. They hadn't given their telephone numbers either. Later there had been calls from Stockholm and from the Swedish Embassy. Then, however, both messages and telephone numbers had been left. They were still here. Would Mr. Beck like to see them? No, Mr. Beck would not like to see them.

The luggage was indeed to be found in a room behind the reception desk. It was very easily inspected. A portable typewriter of the standard make Erika and a yellowish-brown pigskin suitcase with a strap around it. A calling card was fitted into the leather label dangling from the handle. Alf Matsson, Reporter, Fleminggatan 34, Stockholm K. The key was in the lock.

Martin Beck took the typewriter out of its case and studied it for a long time. Having come to the conclusion that it was a portable typewriter of the Erika make, he went over to the suitcase.

The bag appeared neatly and carefully packed, but all the same he had a feeling that someone with a practiced hand had been through it and put everything back into place. The contents consisted of a checked shirt, a brown sport shirt, a white poplin shirt with the laundry band still around it, a pair of freshly pressed light-blue trousers, a kind of blue cardigan, three handkerchiefs, four pairs of socks, two pairs of colored shorts, a fishnet undershirt and a pair of light-brown suede shoes. Everything was clean. In addition, a shaving kit, a sheaf of typing paper, a typewriter eraser, an electric razor, a novel and a dark-blue plastic wallet of the kind that travel agencies usually give away free and that aren't big enough for the tickets. In the shaving kit were shaving lotion, talcum powder, a cake of soap still in its wrapper, a tube of toothpaste that had been opened, a toothbrush, a bottle of mouthwash, a box of aspirin and a pack of contraceptives. In the dark-blue plastic wallet were $1500 in $20 bills and six Swedish 100-kronor notes. An astonishingly large sum for traveling money, but Alf Matsson seemed to be accustomed to doing things in a grand manner.

Martin Beck put everything back as nicely and neatly as possible and returned to the reception desk. It was noon and high time to go out. As he still didn't know what he should do, he might at least do it out in the fresh air—for instance, in the sun on the quay. He took his room key out of his pocket and looked at it. It looked just as old, as venerable and as solid as the hotel itself. He put it down on the desk. The porter at once reached out his hand for the key.

"That's a spare key, isn't it?"

"I don't understand," said the porter.

"I thought that the previous guest took the key with him."

"Yes, that's right. But we got the key back the next day."

"Got it back? Who from?"

"From the police, sir."

"From the police? Which police?"

The porter shrugged his shoulders in bewilderment.

"From the ordinary police, of course. Who else? A policeman handed in the key to the doorman. Mr. Matsson must have dropped it somewhere."

"Where?"

"I'm afraid I don't know, sir."

Martin Beck asked one more question.

"Has anyone else besides me gone through Mr. Matsson's luggage?"

The porter hesitated for a moment before answering.

"I don't think so, sir."

Martin Beck went through the revolving door. The man with the gray mustache and a visored cap was standing in the shade beneath the balcony, perfectly still with his hands behind his back, a living memorial to Emil Jannings.

"Do you remember receiving a room key from a policeman two weeks ago?"

The old man looked at him questioningly.

"Of course."

"Was it a uniformed policeman?"

"Yes, yes . . . A patrol car stopped here and one of the policemen got out and turned in the key."

"What did he say?"

The man thought.

"He said: 'Lost property.' Nothing else, I believe."

Martin Beck turned around and walked away. After three steps, he remembered that he had forgotten to leave a tip. He went back and placed a number of the unfamiliar light-metal coins into the man's hand. The doorman touched the visor of his cap with the fingertips of his right hand and said, "Thank you, but it isn't necessary."

"You speak excellent German," said Martin Beck.

And he thought: Hell of a lot better than I do, anyway.

"I learned it at the Isonzo front in 1916."

As Martin Beck turned the corner of the block, he took out the map and looked at it. Then he walked, map still in hand, down toward the quay. A big white paddle steamer with two funnels was forging its way upriver. He looked at it joylessly.

There was something fundamentally wrong with all this. Something was quite definitely not as it should be. What it was he did not know.

9

It was Sunday and very warm. A light haze of heat trembled over the mountain slopes. The quay was crowded with people walking back and forth or sitting sunning themselves on the steps down to the river. On the small steamers and motor launches shuttling up and down the river people clad in summer clothes crowded together on their way to bathing sites and holiday spots. Long lines were waiting at the ticket offices.

Martin Beck had forgotten that it was Sunday and was at first surprised by the crowds. He followed the stream of strollers and walked along the quay, watching the lively boat traffic. He had thought of starting the day with a walk across the next bridge to Margaret Island, out in the middle of the river, but changed his mind when he imagined the crowds of Budapest citizens spending their Sunday out there.

He was slightly irritated by the crush, and the sight of all these people, happy on their free Sunday, filled him with an urge for activity. He would visit the hotel at which Alf Matsson spent his first and perhaps only night in Budapest—a young people's hotel on the Buda side, the Embassy man had said.

Martin Beck broke out of the stream of people and went up to the street above the quay. He stood in the shade of the gable of a house and studied the map. He hunted for a long time, but could not find a hotel called Ifjuság, and finally he folded up the map and began to walk toward the bridge over to the island and onto the Buda side. He looked around for a police patrolman but did not succeed in finding one. At the end of the bridge there was a taxi stand and a taxi was waiting there. It looked free.

The driver could speak only Hungarian and did not understand a word until Martin Beck showed him the piece of paper with the hotel's name written on it.

They drove across the bridge, past the green island, where he caught sight of a high-flung surge of water between the trees, then on along a shopping street, up steep narrow streets and in onto an open square with lawns and a modernistic bronze group representing a man and a woman sitting staring at each other.

The taxi stopped there and Martin Beck paid—probably much too much, for the driver thanked him profusely in his incomprehensible language.

The hotel was low and spread out along the square, which was more like a widening of the street, with flower beds and parking places. The building appeared to be built just recently, in contrast to the other houses that surrounded the square. The architecture was modern and the entire façade was covered with balconies. The steps leading up to the entrance were wide and few.

Inside the glass doors was a long, light foyer, containing a souvenir stand (which was closed), elevator doors, a couple of groups of chairs and a reception desk. The reception desk was empty and there was not a soul in the foyer.

Adjoining the foyer was a big lounge with armchairs and low tables and large windows all along the far wall. This room was empty too.

Martin Beck went across to the wall with the windows and looked out.

A few young people were lying on the lawn outside, sunning themselves in bathing suits.

The hotel was situated on a hill with a view across to the Pest side. The houses on the slope between the hotel and the river appeared old and shabby. From the taxi Martin Beck had seen bullet holes in most of the façades, and on a number of houses the plastering had been almost entirely shot away.

He looked out into the foyer, which was still just as deserted, and sat down in one of the armchairs in the lounge. He did not expect much from his visit to the Ifjúság. Alf Matsson had stayed here one night, there was a shortage of hotel rooms in Budapest in the summer, and the fact that this particular hotel had a room free was probably sheer chance. It was hardly plausible that anyone would remember a guest who had come late in the evening and left the next morning, at the height of the summer season.

He extinguished his last Florida cigarette and looked gloomily at the sunburned youngsters out on the lawn. It suddenly seemed to him quite ridiculous that he should be gadding about Budapest trying to find a person to whom he was completely indifferent. He could not remember ever being given such a hopeless, meaningless assignment.

Steps could be heard out in the foyer, and Martin Beck got up and went out after them. A young man was standing behind the reception desk with a telephone receiver in his hand, staring up at the ceiling and biting his thumbnail as he listened. Then he began to speak and at first Martin Beck thought the man was speaking Finnish, but then remembered that Finnish and Hungarian stemmed from the same linguistic stock.

The young man put down the receiver and looked inquiringly at Martin Beck, who hesitated while trying to decide which language he should begin with.

"What can I do for you?" said the youth in perfect English, to Martin Beck's relief.

"It's about a guest who stayed at this hotel the night of July twenty-second. Have you any idea who was on duty here that night?"

The young man looked at a wall calendar.

"I really don't remember," he said. "It's more than two weeks ago. One moment, and I'll have a look."

He hunted around for a while on a shelf under the desk, retrieved a little black book and leafed through it. Then he said, "It was me, in fact. Friday night, yes . . . What kind of person? Did he stay just one night?"

"Yes, as far as I know," said Martin Beck. "He might have stayed here later, of course. A Swedish journalist named Alf Matsson."

The youth stared at the ceiling and chewed his nail. Then he shook his head.

"I can't remember any Swede. We get very few Swedes here. What did he look like?"

Martin Beck showed him Alf Matsson's passport photograph. The youth looked at it for a moment and said hesitantly, "I don't know. Perhaps I've seen him before. I can't really remember."

"Do you have a ledger? A guest register?"

The young man pulled out a card-file drawer and began to search. Martin Beck waited. He felt an urge to smoke and hunted through his pockets, but his cigarettes were irrevocably at an end.

"Here it is," said the youth, taking a card out of the drawer. "Alf Matsson. Swedish, yes. He stayed here the night of July twenty-second, just as you say."

"And he didn't stay here after that night?"

"No, not afterward. But he did stay here for a few days at the end of May. But that was before I came here. I was taking my exams then."

Martin Beck took the card and looked at it. Alf Matsson had stayed at the hotel from the twenty-fifth to the twenty-eighth of May.

"Who was on duty here then?"

The youth thought about it. Then he said, "It must have been Stefi. Or else the man who was here before me. I really can't remember what his name is."

"Stefi," said Martin Beck. "Does he still work here?"

"She," said the young man. "It's a girl—Stefania. Yes, she and I work in shifts."

"When is she coming in?"

"She's bound to be here already. I mean in her room. She lives here at the hotel, you see. But she has the night shift this week, so she's probably asleep."

"Could you find out?" asked Martin Beck. "If she's awake, I'd like to speak to her."

The youth lifted the receiver and dialed a number. After a while he replaced the receiver.

"No answer."

He lifted the flap door in the desk and came out.

"I'll see if she's in," he said. "Just a moment."

He got into one of the elevators and Martin Beck saw from the signal light that he had stopped at the second floor. After a while he came down again.

"Her roommate says she's out sunbathing. Wait a moment and I'll go get her."

He disappeared into the lounge and returned a moment later with a girl. She was small and chubby, wearing sandals on her feet and a checkered cotton robe over her bikini. She was buttoning up the robe as she came toward Martin Beck.

"I'm sorry to bother you," he said.

"It doesn't matter," said the girl called Stefi. "Can I help you with anything?"

Martin Beck asked her if she had been on duty during the particular days in May. She went behind the desk, looked in the black book and nodded.

"Yes," she said. "But only in the daytime."

Martin Beck showed her Alf Matsson's passport.

"Swedish?" she asked without looking up.

"Yes," said Martin Beck. "A journalist."

He looked at her and waited. She looked at the passport photograph and cocked her head.

"Ye-es," she said hesitantly. "Yes, I think I remember him. He was alone at first in a room with three beds, and then we had a Russian party, so I needed the room and had to move him. He was awfully angry that he didn't get a telephone in the new room. We haven't got telephones in all the rooms. He made such a fuss about not having one, I was forced to let him exchange rooms with someone who didn't need a telephone."

She closed the passport and put it down on the desk.

"If it was him," she said, "that photo's not very good."

"Do you remember if he had any visitors?" said Martin Beck.

"No," she said. "I don't think so. Not so far as I can remember, anyhow."

"Did he use the phone a lot? Or did he receive any calls which you can remember?"

"It seems to me that a lady rang several times, but I'm not certain," said Stefi.

Martin Beck pondered awhile and then said, "Do you remember anything else about him?"

The girl shook her head.

"He had a typewriter with him, I'm sure. And I remember that he was well dressed. Otherwise I can't remember anything special about him."

Martin Beck put the passport back in his pocket and recalled that he had run out of cigarettes.

"May I buy a pack of cigarettes here?" he said.

The girl bent forward and looked in a drawer.

"Certainly," she said. "But I've only got Tervs."

"That's fine," said Martin Beck, taking the pack made of gray paper, with a picture of a factory with tall smokestacks on it. He paid with a note and told her to keep the change. Then he took a pen and a pad from the desk, wrote down his own name and that of his hotel, tore off the sheet and handed it to Stefi.

"If you can think of anything else, perhaps you'd call me, would you?"

Stefi looked at the piece of paper with a frown.

"I've just remembered something else when you were writing that note," she said. "I think it was that Swede who asked how you got to an address in Újpest. It might not have been him,

I'm not certain. Perhaps it was a different guest. I drew a little map for him."

She fell silent and Martin Beck waited.

"I remember the street he was asking about, but not the number. My aunt lives on that street, so that's why I remembered it."

Martin Beck pushed the pad toward her.

"Would you be good enough to write down the name of the street for me?"

As Martin Beck came out of the hotel, he looked at the slip of paper. Venetianer út.

He put the paper into his pocket, lit a Terv and began strolling down toward the river.

10

It was Monday the eighth of August and Martin Beck was waked by the telephone. He propped himself sleepily up on his elbow, fumbled with the receiver a moment and heard the telephone operator say something he did not understand. Then a familiar voice said:

"Hullo."

Out of sheer astonishment, Martin Beck forgot to reply.

"Hulloo-o-o, is anyone there?"

Kollberg could be heard as clearly as if he had been in the room next door.

"Where are you?"

"At the office, of course. It's already quarter past nine. Don't tell me you're still lying snoring in bed."

"What's the weather like up your way?" said Martin Beck, then falling silent, paralyzed himself by the idiocy of the remark.

"It's raining," said Kollberg suspiciously, "but that wasn't why I called. Are you sick or something?"

Martin Beck managed to sit up on the edge of the bed and light one of those unfamiliar Hungarian cigarettes from the pack with the factory on it.

"No. What d'you want?"

"I've been digging around a bit up here. Alf Matsson doesn't seem to be a very nice guy."

"How so?"

"Well. Mostly just an impression I've got. He just seems to be one big all-round ass."

"Did you call to tell me that?"

"No, actually, I didn't. But there was one thing I thought you ought to know. I didn't have anything to do on Saturday so I went and sat around in that bar place. The Tankard."

"Listen, don't go poking your nose in too much. Officially you've never even heard about this case. And you don't know I'm here."

Kollberg sounded clearly offended.

"D'you think I'm a moron?"

"Only occasionally," said Martin Beck, amiably.

"I didn't speak to anyone. Just sat at the table next to that gang and listened to them shoot the breeze. For five hours. They sure put away the liquor."

The telephone operator broke in and said something incomprehensible.

"You're bankrupting the government," said Martin Beck. "What's up? Get it off your chest."

"Well, the guys were shooting the bull back and forth, one thing and another about Alfie, as they call him. They're just the type to let off a lot of hot air behind each other's backs. As soon as one of them goes to the head, then the others all get started on him."

"Don't be so long-winded."

"That Molin seems to be the worst. He was the one who started talking about the thing I'm calling about, too. Nasty, but it might not be *all* lies."

"Come on now, look sharp, Lennart."

"And *you* tell me that! Anyhow it turned out that Matsson

makes off like a shot for Hungary because he's got a gal down there. Some sort of small-time athlete he met while he was a sports reporter here in Stockholm—at some international sports meet or other. While he was still living with his wife."

"Uh-huh."

"They also said it was very likely that he arranged his trips to other places—Prague and Berlin and so forth—so he could meet her when she was competing there."

"Doesn't sound likely to me. Girl athletes are usually kept under lock and key."

"Take it for what it's worth."

"Thanks," said Martin Beck, without a trace of enthusiasm. "So long."

"Wait a second. I haven't finished yet. They never mentioned her name—I don't think they even knew it. But they gave enough details for me to be able to . . . It rained yesterday too."

"Lennart," said Martin Beck desperately.

"I managed to force my way into the Royal Library and sat all day yesterday looking through back numbers. As far as I can make out, it can only be a gal named—I'll spell it."

Martin Beck switched on the bedside lamp and wrote the letters on the edge of the map of Budapest. A-R-I B-Ö-K-K.

"Got it?" said Kollberg.

"Of course."

"She's German actually, but a Hungarian citizen. Don't know where she lives, nor that the spelling's quite right. Not very famous. I couldn't think of any name that reminded me of hers in any connection since May of last year. Apparently she was some kind of substitute. On the second team."

"Have you finished now?"

"One more thing. His car is where it ought to be. In the airport parking place here at Arlanda. An Opel Rekord. Nothing special about it."

"Really. Have you finished now?"

"Yes."

"G'bye, then."

"Bye."

Martin Beck stared listlessly at the letters he had written down. Ari Bökk. It did not even look like the name of a human being. Probably the particulars were wrong and the information completely useless.

He got up, opened the shutters and let in the summer. The view over the river and the Buda side was just as fascinating as it had been twenty-four hours ago. The Czech paddle steamer had left, making way for a propeller-driven motor vessel with two low funnels. It was Czechoslovakian too and was called *Druzba*. People dressed for summer were sitting eating breakfast at the tables in front of the hotel. It was already half past nine. He felt useless and negligent of his duties, so he swiftly washed and dressed, put the map in his pocket and hurried downstairs to the vestibule. Having hurried all the way down, he then remained standing absolutely motionless. To hurry seemed pointless when you didn't know what to do when you got there anyway. He meditated on this for a moment, then went into the dining room, sat down by one of the open windows and had breakfast served to him. Boats of every size were passing by. A large Soviet tugboat towing three oil barges worked its way upstream. Presumably it came from Batum. That was a long way away. The captain was wearing a white cap. The waiters swarmed around Martin Beck's table as if he were Rockefeller. Small boys were kicking a ball on the street. A big dog wanted to join in and almost knocked over the well-dressed lady holding its leash. She had to grab hold of one of the stone pillars of the balustrade to keep from falling. After a while she let go of the pillar but retained her hold on the leash, running, at a sharp backward tilt behind the dog, in among the ballplayers. It was already very warm. The river sparkled.

His lack of constructive ideas was conspicuous. Martin Beck turned his head and saw a person staring at him: a sunburned man of his own age, with graying hair, straight nose, brown eyes, gray suit, black shoes, white shirt and gray tie. He had a large signet ring on the little finger of his right hand and beside him on the table lay a speckled green hat with a narrow brim and a fluffy little feather in the band. The man returned to his double espresso.

Martin Beck moved his eyes and saw a woman staring at him. She was African and young and very beautiful, with clean features, large brilliant eyes, white teeth, long slim legs and high insteps. Silver sandals and a tight-fitting light-blue dress of some shiny material.

Presumably they were both staring at Martin Beck—the man with envy, the woman with ill-concealed desire—because he was so handsome.

Martin Beck sneezed and three waiters blessed him. He thanked them, went out into the vestibule, took the map out of his pocket and showed the letters he had written on it to the porter.

"Do you know of anybody by this name?"

"No sir."

"It's supposed to be some kind of sports star."

"Really?"

The porter looked politely sympathetic. Naturally, a guest was always right.

"Perhaps not so well known, sir."

"Is it a man's or a woman's name?"

"Ari is a woman's name—almost a nickname. A different version of Aranka, for children."

The porter cocked his head and looked at the words.

"But the last name, sir. Is it really a name?"

"May I borrow a telephone directory?"

Naturally there was no one called Bökk, anyhow no human being. But he didn't give up that easily. (A cheap virtue when a person still doesn't know what to do.) He tried several other possibilities. The result was as follows: BOECK ESZTER penzió XII Venetianer út 6 292-173.

Struck by his first thought of the day, he took out the slip of paper he had received from the girl at the young people's hotel. Venetianer út. It could hardly be a coincidence.

At the reception desk a young lady had taken the august old porter's place.

"What does this mean?"

"*Penzió*. Pension—boarding house. Shall I call the number for you?"

He shook his head.

"Where is this street?"

"The Fourth District. In Újpest."

"How do you get there?"

"It's quickest by taxi, of course. Otherwise, Trolley Line Three from Marx Square. But it's more comfortable to take one of the boats that tie up outside here. Heading north."

11

The boat was called *Úttörő* and was a joy to the eye. A little coal-fired steamer with a tall, straight funnel and open decks. As it calmly and comfortably chugged up the river past the Parliament building and green Margaret Island, Martin Beck stood at the railing philosophizing about the accursed cult of the combustion engine. He walked over to the engine room and peered down. The heat came out like a column from the boiler room. The fireman was dressed in bathing trunks, and his muscular back was shiny with sweat. The coal shovel rattled. What was this man thinking about down in that infernal heat? In all probability, about the blessing of the combustion engine: he no doubt saw himself sitting reading the newspaper beside a diesel engine, cotton waste and an oil can within easy reach. Martin Beck returned to studying the boat, but the fireman had spoiled his enjoyment. It was the same with most things. You couldn't have your cake and eat it too.

The boat slid past spacious, open-air parks and bathing places, edged its way through a swarm of canoes and pleasure boats, passed two bridges and continued through a narrow sound into quite a small tributary of the river. It gave a short hoarse toot of triumph and tied up in Újpest.

After Martin Beck had gone ashore, he turned around and looked at the steamer, so exquisite in form and so functional—in its day. The fireman came up on deck, laughed at the sun and leaped straight into the water.

This part of the city was of a different character from the sections of Budapest he had seen previously. He walked diagonally across the large, bare square and made a few feeble attempts to ask his way, but could not make himself understood. Despite the map, he went astray and wound up in a yard behind a synagogue, evidently a home for elderly Jews. Frail survivors from the days of great evil nodded cheerfully at him from their wicker chairs in the narrow strip of shade along the walls.

Five minutes later he was standing outside the building Venetianer út Number 6. It was built in two stories and nothing about its exterior gave the impression that it was a boarding house, but out on the street stood two cars with foreign license plates. He met the landlady as soon as he got into the hall.

"Frau Boeck?"

"Yes—we're full up I'm afraid."

She was a stout woman of fifty years. Her German sounded extraordinarily fluent.

"I am looking for a lady named Ari Boeck."

"That's my niece. One flight up. Second door to the right."

With that, she went away. Simple as that. Martin Beck stood for a moment outside the white-painted door and heard someone moving about inside. Then he knocked quite lightly. The door was opened at once.

"Fräulein Boeck?"

The woman seemed surprised. Very likely, she had been

expecting someone. She was wearing a dark-blue, two-piece bathing suit and in her right hand she was carrying a green rubber diving mask and a snorkel. She was standing with her feet wide apart and her left hand still on the lock, quite still, as if paralyzed in the middle of a movement. Her hair was dark and short, and her features were strong. She had thick black eyebrows, a broad straight nose and full lips. Her teeth were good but somewhat uneven. Her mouth was half-open and the tip of her tongue was resting against her lower teeth, as if she was just about to say something. She was hardly taller than five foot one, but strongly and harmoniously built, with well-developed shoulders, broad hips and quite a narrow waist. Her legs were muscular and her feet short and broad, with straight toes. She had a very deep suntan and her skin appeared soft and elastic, especially across her diaphragm and stomach. Shaved armpits. Large breasts and curved stomach with thick down that seemed very light against her tanned skin. Here and there, long and curly black hairs had made their way out from under the elastic at her loins. She might have been twenty-two or twenty-three years old, at the most. Not beautiful in the conventional sense of the word, but a highly functional specimen of the human race.

A questioning look in large, dark-brown eyes. Finally she said, "Yes, that's me. Were you looking for me?"

Not quite such fluent German as her aunt's, but almost.

"I'm looking for Alf Matsson."

"Who is that?"

Her general attitude was that of a child in a state of shock. It made him incapable of discerning any definite reaction to the name. Quite possibly it was completely new to her.

"A Swedish journalist. From Stockholm."

"Is he supposed to be living here? There's no Swede here at the moment. You must have made a mistake."

She thought for a moment, frowning.

"But how did you know my name?"

The room behind her was an ordinary boarding-house room. Clothes lay carelessly strewn about on the furniture. Only women's clothing, as far as he could see.

"He gave me this address himself. Matsson is a friend of mine."

She looked suspiciously at him and said: "How odd."

He took the passport out of his pocket and turned to the page with Matsson's photo on it. She looked at it carefully.

"No. I've never seen him before."

After a while she said, "Have you lost each other?"

Before Martin Beck had time to reply, he heard a padding sound behind him and took a step to one side. A man in his thirties went past him into the room. Wearing bathing trunks, below average height, blond, very strongly built, with the same formidable tan as the woman. The man took a position behind her and to one side and peered inquisitively at the passport.

"Who's that?" he said in German.

"I don't know. This gentleman has lost him. Thought he'd moved here."

"Lost," said the blond man. "That's not good. And without his passport too. I know what a bother that can be. I'm in that line myself."

Playfully, he pulled the elastic of the woman's bathing suit as far as he could and let it go with a smack. She gave him a quick look of annoyance.

"Aren't we going out for a swim?" said the man.

"Yes, I'm ready."

"Ari Boeck," said Martin Beck. "I recognize the name. Aren't you the swimmer?"

For the first time, the girl's eyes wavered.

"I don't compete any longer."

"Haven't you done some swimming in Sweden?"

"Yes, once. Two years ago. I was last. Funny that he gave you my address."

The blond man looked inquiringly at her. No one said anything. Martin Beck put the passport away.

"Well, good-bye, then. Sorry to have troubled you."

"Good-bye," said the woman, smiling for the first time.

"Hope you find your friend," said the blond man. "Have you tried the camping site by the Roman Baths? It's up here, on the other side of the river. A huge number of people there. You can take a boat over."

"You're German, aren't you?"

"Yes, from Hamburg."

The man rumpled the girl's short dark hair. Lightly she brushed his chest with the back of her left hand. Martin Beck turned around and went away.

The entrance hall was empty. On a shelf behind the table that served as a reception desk lay a little stack of passports. The top one was Finnish, but underneath it lay two in that familiar moss-green color. As if in passing, he stretched out his hand and took one of them. He opened it and the man he had met in Ari Boeck's doorway stared glassily up at him. Tetz Radeberger, Travel Agency Official, Hamburg, born in 1935. Evidently no one had taken the trouble to lie to him.

He had bad luck on his journey home and ended up on a modern fast-moving ferryboat with roofed decks and growling diesel engines. There were only a few passengers on board—nearest to him sat two old women in gaudily colored shawls and bright dresses. They were carrying large white bundles and presumably had come from the country. Farther away in the saloon sat a serious, middle-aged man in a brown felt hat who was carrying a briefcase and wearing the facial expression of a civil servant. A tall man in a blue suit was whittling listlessly at a stick. By the landing stage stood a uniformed police officer, eating figure-eight-shaped cookies out of a paper cornet and talking sporadically to a small, well-dressed man with a bald head and a black mustache. A young couple with two doll-like children completed the assemblage.

Martin Beck inspected his fellow passengers gloomily. His expedition had been a failure. There was nothing to indicate that Ari Boeck had not been telling the truth.

Inwardly he cursed the strange impulse that had made him take on this pointless assignment. The possibilities of his solving the case became more and more remote. He was alone and without an idea in his head. And if, on the other hand, he had had any ideas, he would have lacked resources to implement them.

The worst of it was that, deep down within himself, he knew that he had not been guided by any kind of impulse at all. It was just his policeman's soul—or whatever it might be called—that had started to function. It was the same instinct that made Kollberg sacrifice his time off—a kind of occupational disease that forced him to take on all assignments and do his best to solve them.

When he got back to the hotel it was a quarter past four and the dining room was closed. He had missed lunch. He went up to his room, showered and put on his dressing gown. Taking a pull of whisky from the bottle he had bought on the plane, he found the taste raw and unpleasant and went out to the bathroom to brush his teeth. Then he leaned out the window, his elbows resting on the wide window sill, and watched the boats. Not even that managed to amuse him very much. Directly below him, at one of the outdoor tables, sat one of the passengers on the boat: the man in the blue suit. He had a glass of beer on the table and was still whittling at his stick.

Martin Beck frowned and lay down on the creaking bed. Again he thought the situation over. Sooner or later he would be forced to contact the police. It was a doubtful measure and no one would like it—at this stage not even he himself.

He whiled away the time remaining before dinner by sitting idling in an armchair in the lobby. On the other side of the room a gray-haired man wearing a signet ring was reading a Hungarian newspaper. It was the same man who had stared at him at breakfast. Martin Beck looked at him for a long time, but the man tranquilly went on drinking his coffee and seemed quite unconscious of his surroundings.

Martin Beck dined on mushroom soup and a perch-like fish

from Lake Balaton, washed down felicitously with white wine. The little orchestra played Liszt and Strauss and other composers of that elevated school. It was a superb dinner, but it did not gladden him, and the waiters swarmed around their lugubrious guest like medical experts around a dictator's sickbed.

He had his coffee and brandy in the lobby. The man with the signet ring was still reading his newspaper on the other side of the room. Once again a glass of coffee was standing in front of him. After a few minutes, the man looked at his watch, glanced across at Martin Beck, folded up his paper and walked across the room.

Martin Beck was to be spared the problem of contacting the police. The police had taken that initiative. Twenty-three years' experience had taught him to recognize a policeman from his walk.

12

The man in the gray suit took a calling card out of his top pocket and placed it on the edge of the table. Martin Beck glanced down at it as he rose to his feet. Only a name. Vilmos Szluka.

"May I sit down?"

The man spoke English. Martin Beck nodded.

"I'm from the police."

"So am I," said Martin Beck.

"I realized that. Coffee?"

Martin Beck nodded. The man from the police held up two fingers and almost immediately a waiter hurried forward with two glasses. This was clearly a coffee-drinking nation.

"I also realize that you are here to make certain investigations."

Martin Beck did not reply immediately. He rubbed his nose and thought. Obviously this was the right moment to say, "Not at all—I'm here as a tourist, but I'm trying to get hold of a friend I'd like to see." That was presumably what was expected of him.

Szluka did not seem to be in any special hurry. With obvious pleasure he sipped at his double espresso, however many that made now. Martin Beck had seen him drink at least three earlier in the day. The man was behaving politely but formally. His eyes were friendly, but very professional.

Martin Beck went on pondering. This man was indeed a policeman, but so far as he knew there was no law in the whole world that said that individual citizens should tell the police the truth. Unfortunately.

"Yes," said Martin Beck. "That's correct."

"Then wouldn't the most logical thing to do have been to turn to us first?"

Martin Beck preferred not to reply to that one. After a pause of a few seconds, the other man developed the train of thought himself.

"In the event something that demands an investigation really should have happened," he said.

"I have no official assignment."

"And we have not been notified of any charge. Only an inquiry in very vague terms. In other words, it appears that nothing has happened."

Martin Beck gulped down his coffee, which was extremely strong. The conversation was growing more unpleasant than he had expected. But under any circumstances, there was no reason for him to allow himself to be lectured to in a hotel foyer by a policeman who did not even take the trouble to identify himself.

"Nonetheless, the police here have considered that they had cause to go through Alf Matsson's belongings," he said.

It was a random comment but it struck home.

"I don't know anything about that," said Szluka stiffly. "Can you identify yourself, by the way?"

"Can you?"

He caught a swift change in those brown eyes. The man was by no means harmless.

Szluka put his hand into his inside pocket, withdrew his wallet and opened it, swiftly and casually. Martin Beck did not bother to look, but showed his service badge clipped to his key ring.

"That's not valid identification," said Szluka. "In our country you can buy emblems of different kinds in the toyshops."

This point of view was not entirely without justification and Martin Beck did not consider the matter worth further argument. He took out his identification card.

"My passport is at the reception desk."

The other man studied the card thoroughly and at length. As he returned it, he said, "How long are you planning to stay?"

"My visa is good until the end of the month."

Szluka smiled for the first time during their conversation. The smile hardly came from the heart and it was not difficult to figure out what it meant. The Hungarian sipped up the last drop of coffee, buttoned up his jacket and said:

"I do not wish to stop you although, naturally, I could do it. As far as I can see, your activities are more or less of a private nature. I assume that they will remain so and that they will not harm the interests of the general public or any individual citizen."

"You can always go on tailing me, of course."

Szluka did not reply. His eyes were cold and hostile.

"What do you really think you're doing?" he said.

"What do *you* think?"

"I don't know. Nothing has happened."

"Only that a person has disappeared."

"Who says so?"

"I do."

"In that case you should go to the authorities and demand that the case be investigated in the ordinary way," said Szluka stiffly.

Martin Beck drummed on the table with his fingers.

"The man is missing—there's no doubt about it."

The other man was evidently just about to leave. He was sitting absolutely upright in the easychair, with his right hand on the arm.

"By that statement you actually mean—as far as I can make out—that the person in question has not been seen here at this hotel during the last two weeks. He has a valid residence permit and can travel freely within the country's borders. At present there are a couple hundred thousand tourists here, many of them spending their nights in tents or sleeping in their cars. This man might be in Szeged or Debrecen. He might have gone to Lake Balaton to spend his holiday bathing."

"Alf Matsson did not come here to swim."

"Is that so? In any case, he has a tourist visa. Why should he disappear, as you call it? Had he, for instance, booked his return ticket?"

The last question was worthy of some thought. The manner in which it was put indicated that the man already knew the answer. Szluka rose to his feet.

"Just a moment," said Martin Beck. "I'd like to ask you about one thing."

"Please go ahead. What do you want to know?"

"When Alf Matsson left the hotel, he took his room key with him. The next day, it was handed in here by a uniformed policeman. Where did the police get the key from?"

Szluka looked straight at him for at least fifteen seconds. Then he said, "Unfortunately, I cannot answer that question. Good-bye."

He walked swiftly through the lobby, stopped at the coat-check counter, received his gray-brown hat with a feather in it and stood with it in his hand, as if thinking about something. Then he turned around and went back to Martin Beck's table.

"Here is your passport."

"Thank you."

"It wasn't at the reception desk, as you thought. You were mistaken."

"Yes," said Martin Beck.

He found nothing amusing about the other man's behavior and did not bother to look up. Szluka remained standing there.

"What do you think of the food here?" he said.

"It's good."

"I'm delighted to hear it."

The Hungarian said this as if he really meant it, and Martin Beck raised his head.

"You see," explained Szluka, "nothing very dramatic or exciting happens here nowadays—it's not like in your country or in London or New York."

The combination was somewhat bewildering.

"We've had more than enough of that in the past," said Szluka solemnly. "Now we want peace and quiet, and we take an interest in other things. Food, for instance. I myself had four slices of fat bacon and two fried eggs for breakfast. And for lunch I had fish soup and fried, breaded carp. Apple strudel for dessert."

He paused. Then he said thoughtfully, "The children don't like fat bacon, of course. They usually have cocoa and buttered sweet rolls before they go to school."

"Uh-huh."

"Yes. And this evening I'm going to have veal schnitzel with rice and paprika sauce. Not bad. Have you tasted the fish soup here, by the way?"

"No."

Indeed, he had come across this fish soup on his first evening, but he could not see that this had anything to do with the Hungarian police.

"You definitely ought to try it. It's excellent. But it's even better at Matya's, a place quite near here. You ought to take the time to go there—like most of the other foreigners."

"Uh-huh."

"But I can assure you that I know a place where they have

even better fish soup. The best fish soup in all Budapest. It's a little place up on Lajos út. Not many tourists find their way there. You have to go down to Szeged to find a soup like this."

"Uh-huh."

Szluka had become noticeably exhilarated during this report on culinary matters. He appeared to be collecting his thoughts now and looked at his watch. Presumably he was thinking about his veal schnitzel.

"Have you had time to see anything of Budapest?"

"A little. It's a beautiful city."

"Yes, it is, isn't it? Have you been to the Palatine Baths?"

"No."

"They're worth a visit. I'm planning to go there myself tomorrow. Perhaps we could go together."

"Why not?"

"Excellent. In that case I'll meet you at two o'clock outside the entrance."

"Good-bye."

Martin Beck remained seated awhile, thinking. The conversation had been unpleasant and disquieting. Szluka's last sudden change in attitude did not in any way alter that impression. More intensely than ever, he had a feeling that something did not fit, and at the same time, his own impotence seemed more and more apparent.

At about half past eleven, the foyer and the dining room began to empty and Martin Beck went up to his room. After he had undressed, he stood for a moment by the open window, inhaling the warm night air. A paddle steamer slid by on the river, brightly illuminated with green, red and yellow lights. People were dancing on the aft deck and the sound of the music came through intermittently across the water.

A few people were still sitting at the tables in front of the hotel, one of them a tall man in his thirties, with dark wavy hair. The man had a glass of beer in front of him and had obviously been home and exchanged his blue suit for a light-gray one.

He shut the window and went to bed. Then he lay in the dark thinking: the police may not be especially interested in Alf Matsson, but they're certainly interested in Martin Beck.

It was a long time before he fell asleep.

13

Martin Beck sat in the shade by the stone balustrade in front of the hotel, eating a late breakfast. It was his third day in Budapest and it promised to be just as warm and beautiful as the previous ones.

Breakfast was nearly over, and he and an elderly couple, who sat in silence a few tables away, were the only guests. There were a good many people moving about on the street and down on the quay, mostly mothers with children and low streamlined baby carriages like small white tanks.

The tall dark man with a stick was not visible, which in itself did not necessarily mean that he was no longer being watched. The police corps was large and there were no doubt replacements.

A waiter came over and cleared his table.

"Frühstück nicht gut?"

He looked unhappily at the untouched salami.

Martin Beck assured him that the breakfast had been very good. When the waiter had gone away, he took out a picture postcard he had bought in the hotel kiosk. It was of a paddle steamer on its way up the Danube, with one of the bridges in the background. The lady in the kiosk had stamped the card for him and he pondered for a moment over whom he should send it to. Then he addressed it to Gunnar Ahlberg, Police Station, Motala, wrote a few words of greetings on it, and put it back into his pocket.

He had met Ahlberg two summers ago, when the body of a

woman had been found in the Göta Canal at Motala. They had become good friends during the six-month investigation and had kept in touch sporadically ever since. At the time the investigation and search for the murderer had become a personal affair for him. It had not been only the policeman in him that caused him to think of nothing else but the case for months on end.

And now, here in Budapest, it was only with the greatest effort that he could summon up any interest for his assignment.

Martin Beck felt stupidly useless as he sat there. He had several hours to dispose of before his meeting with Szluka, and the only constructive thing he could think of doing was putting the postcard to Ahlberg into the mailbox. It annoyed him that Szluka had asked him (before he had thought of it himself) whether he had checked to see if Matsson had booked a return flight. He took out his map and found one of the airline's branch offices near a square close to the hotel. Afterward he got up, walked through the dining room and the foyer, and put the postcard in the red mailbox outside the hotel entrance. Then he began walking in toward town.

The square was large, with shops and travel agencies and a great deal of traffic. Many people were already sitting at a sidewalk café, drinking coffee at the small tables. Outside this café he saw a stairway that led down underneath the street. "Földalatti" appeared on a sign and he supposed that the word meant W. C. He felt sticky and warm and decided to go down there and wash before he visited the airline office. He crossed the street diagonally and followed two gentlemen carrying briefcases down underground.

He descended into the smallest subway he had ever seen. On the platform was a little glassed-in wooden kiosk painted green and white, and the low roof was held up by decorative cast-iron pillars. The train, which was already standing there, looked more like a dwarf-sized train at an amusement park than an efficient means of transportation. He remembered that this subway was the oldest in Europe.

He paid the fare, and got a ticket at the kiosk and stepped into the little varnished wooden car—it could well have been the same one Emperor Frans Joseph had traveled in when he had opened the line some time at the end of the previous century. There was a pause before the doors closed, and the car was full as the train started.

On the small platform in the middle of the car stood three men and a woman. They were deaf-mutes and were carrying on a lively conversation in sign language. When the train stopped for the third time, they got off, still eagerly gesticulating. Before the platform filled up again, Martin Beck had time to notice a man sitting at the other end of the car, half-turned away from him.

The man was dark and sunburned and Martin Beck recognized him at once. Instead of the gray jacket he was now wearing a green shirt, open at the neck. There was probably nothing left of the stick he had been whittling on all the previous day.

Suddenly the train plunged out of the tunnel and slowed down. It rode on into a green park with a big pool, shimmering in the sunlight. Then it stopped and the car emptied. This was evidently the end of the line.

The last to step out of the car, Martin Beck looked around for the dark man. He was nowhere to be seen.

A wide road led into the park, which looked cool and inviting, but Martin Beck decided against any further expeditions. He read the timetable on the platform and saw that the stretch between this park and the square where he had got on was the only line and that the train would be returning in a quarter of an hour.

It was half past eleven when he went into Malev's office. The five girls behind the counter were busy with customers, so Martin Beck sat down by the street window to wait.

He had not succeeded in spotting the man with the dark wavy hair on his return from the park, but he presumed that he was still somewhere in the vicinity. He wondered whether he would be tailing him during his meeting with Szluka too.

One of the chairs by the counter became free and Martin Beck went up to it and sat down. The girl behind the counter had her dark hair done in an elaborate set of curls on her forehead. She looked efficient and was smoking a cigarette with a scarlet filter tip.

Martin Beck carried out his errand. Had a Swedish journalist by the name of Alf Matsson booked a flight to Stockholm or anywhere else after the twenty-third of July?

The girl offered him a cigarette and began leafing through her papers. After a while she picked up the telephone and spoke to someone, shook her head and went over to speak to one of her colleagues.

After all five of them had leafed through their lists, it was past twelve o'clock and the girl with the curls informed him that no Alf Matsson had booked a flight on any plane leaving Budapest.

Martin Beck decided to skip lunch and went up to his room. He opened the window and looked down onto the lunch guests below. No tall man in a green shirt was visible.

At one of the tables sat six men in their thirties drinking beer. A thought struck him, and he went over to the telephone and set up a call to Stockholm. Then he lay down on the bed and waited.

A quarter of an hour later the phone rang and he heard Kollberg's voice.

"Hi! How's things?"

"Bad."

"Have you found that chick? Bökk?"

"Yes, but it was nothing. She didn't even know who he was. A musclebound blond boy was standing there feeling her up."

"So it was just a lot of big talk then. He was pretty much of a big mouth, according to his so-called buddies here."

"Have you got a lot to do?"

"Nothing at all. I can go on digging around if you like."

"You can do one thing for me. Find out the names of those

guys at the Tankard and what sort of people they are, will you?"

"O.K. Anything else?"

"Be careful. Remember that they probably are journalists, all of them. So long. I'm going swimming now with somebody named Szluka."

"That's a hell of a name for a chick. Martin, listen, have you checked to see if he booked a return flight?"

"Bye," said Martin Beck, and put down the receiver.

He hunted up his bathing trunks from his bag, rolled them up in one of the hotel towels and went down to the boat station.

The boat was called *Óbuda* and one of the unpleasant roofed types. But he was late and it had the advantage of being faster than the coal-fired boats.

He stepped ashore below a large hotel on Margaret Island. Then he followed the road toward the interior of the island, walked swiftly beneath the shady trees along a lush green lawn, past a tennis court, and then he was there.

Szluka was standing waiting outside the entrance, his briefcase in hand. He was dressed as on the previous day.

"I'm sorry to have kept you waiting," said Martin Beck.

"I've just come," said Szluka.

They paid and went into the dressing room. A bald old man in a white undershirt greeted Szluka and unlocked two lockers. Szluka took a pair of black bathing trunks out of his briefcase, swiftly undressed and meticulously hung his clothes on a hanger. They pulled on their bathing trunks simultaneously, although Martin Beck had had considerably fewer garments to remove.

Szluka took his briefcase and went ahead out of the dressing room. Martin Beck followed behind with his towel rolled up in his hand.

The place was full of suntanned people. Immediately in front of the dressing room was a round pool with fountains spouting up tall streams of water. Shrieking children were running in and out under the waterfalls. On one side of the fountain pool was a smaller pool with steps sloping down into the water from one end. On the other was a large pool full of clear green water which darkened toward the middle. This pool was full of swimming and splashing people of all ages. The area between the pools and the lawns was covered with stone slabs.

Martin Beck followed Szluka along the edge of the large pool. In front of them and farther on they could see a semicircular arcade, for which Szluka was evidently heading.

A voice on the loudspeaker called out some information and a mob of people began to run toward the pool with the steps leading down into it. Martin Beck was almost knocked over and followed Szluka's example, stepping to one side until the rush was over. He looked inquiringly at Szluka, who said:

"Wave bathing."

Martin Beck watched the small pool swiftly filling with people, who finally stood packed like sardines. A pair of huge pumps began to swish water toward the high edges of the pool and the human shoal rocked on the high waves, amid cries of delight.

"Perhaps you'd like to go and ride the waves," said Szluka.

Martin Beck looked at him. He was quite serious.

"No, thank you," said Martin Beck.

"Personally, I usually bathe in the sulfur spring," said Szluka. "It is very relaxing."

The spring ran from a stone cairn in the middle of an oval pool—the water was knee-deep there and its far end was shaded by the arcade. The pool was built like a labyrinth, with walls that rose about ten inches above ground level. The walls formed back supports for molded armchairs in which one sat with the water up to one's chin.

Szluka stepped down into the pool and began to wade between the rows of seated people. He was still holding his briefcase in his hand. Martin Beck wondered if he was so used to carrying it that he had forgotten to put it down, but he said nothing and stepped down into the pool and began to wade along at Szluka's heels.

The water was quite warm and the steam smelled of sulfur. Szluka waded into the colonnade, put down his briefcase on the edge of the wall and sat down in the water. Martin Beck sat down beside him. It was very comfortable in the spacious stone armchair, which had broad arms about six inches below the surface of the water.

Szluka leaned his head against the back and closed his eyes. Martin Beck said nothing and looked at the bathers.

Nearly opposite him sat a small, pale, thin man, bouncing a fat blonde on his knee. They were both looking seriously and absent-mindedly at a little girl who was splashing about in front of them with a rubber ring around her stomach.

A pale, freckled boy in white bathing trunks came slowly wading by. Behind him he was towing a sturdy youth by a loose grip on his big toe. The youth was lying on his back, staring up at the sky, his hands clasped over his stomach.

On the edge of the pool stood a tall sunburned man with wavy dark hair. His bathing trunks were pale-blue with wide flapping legs, more like undershorts than trunks. Martin Beck suspected that this was in fact the case. Perhaps he should have warned him that he was going swimming, so that the man would have had time to go and get his trunks.

Suddenly, without opening his eyes, Szluka said, "The key was lying on the steps of the police station. A patrolman found it there."

Martin Beck looked in surprise at Szluka, who was lying utterly relaxed beside him. The hair on his sunburned chest was fluttering slowly about like white seaweed in the shimmering green water.

"How did it get there?"

Szluka turned his head and looked at him beneath half-closed lids.

77

"You won't believe me, of course, but the fact is, I don't know."

A long-drawn-out cry of disappointment, in unison, was heard coming from the smaller pool. The wave bathing was over for this time and the large pool filled up with people again.

"Yesterday you didn't want to tell me where you'd got the key from. Why did you tell me now?" said Martin Beck.

"As you seem to misinterpret most things anyway, and it was a piece of information you could have got hold of elsewhere, I considered it better to tell you myself."

After a while Martin Beck said, "Why are you having me tailed?"

"I don't understand what you're talking about," said Szluka.

"What did you have for lunch?"

"Fish soup and carp," said Szluka.

"And applestrudel?"

"No, wild strawberries and whipped cream and powdered sugar," said Szluka. "Delicious."

Martin Beck looked around. The man in the undershorts had gone.

"When was the key found?" he said.

"The day before it was handed in to the hotel. On the afternoon of the twenty-third of July."

"On the same day that Alf Matsson disappeared, in fact."

Szluka straightened up and looked at Martin Beck. Then he turned around, opened his briefcase, took out a towel and dried his hands. Then he pulled out a file and leafed through it.

"We have made some inquiries, actually" he said, "despite the fact that we have had no official request for an investigation."

He took a paper out of the file and went on, "You seem to be taking this matter more seriously than appears to be necessary. Is he an important person, this Alf Matsson?"

"Insofar as he has disappeared in a way that can't be explained, yes. We consider that sufficiently important grounds to find out what's happened to him."

"What is there to indicate that something has happened to him?"

"Nothing. But the fact is, he's gone."

Szluka looked at his paper.

"According to the passport and customs authorities, no Swedish citizen by the name Alf Matsson has left Hungary since the twenty-second of July. Anyway, he left his passport at the hotel, and he can hardly have left the country without it. No person—known or unknown—who might have been this Alf Matsson has been taken to a hospital or morgue here in this country during the period in question. Without his passport, Matsson cannot have been accepted at any other hotel in the country either. Consequently, everything indicates that for some reason or another your compatriot has made up his mind to stay in Hungary for an additional period."

Szluka put the paper back into the file and closed his briefcase.

"The man's been here before. Perhaps he's acquired some friends and is staying with them," he went on, settling himself down again.

"And yet there's no reasonable explanation for his leaving the hotel and not letting anyone know where he is," said Martin Beck a little later.

Szluka rose and picked up his briefcase.

"So long as he has a valid visa, I cannot—as I said—do anything more in the matter," he said.

Martin Beck also rose.

"Stay where you are," said Szluka. "Unfortunately I have to go. But perhaps we'll meet again. Good-bye."

They shook hands and Martin Beck watched him wading away with his briefcase. From his appearance, one would not think he ate four slices of fat bacon for breakfast.

When Szluka had disappeared, Martin Beck went over to the large pool. The warm water and sulfur fumes had made him drowsy, and he swam around for a while in the clear cooling water before sitting in the sun on the edge of the pool to dry. For a while he watched two deadly serious middle-aged men standing in the shallow end of the pool, tossing a red ball to each other.

Then he went in to change. He felt lost and confused. He was none the wiser for his meeting with Szluka.

14

After his bathe, the heat did not seem quite so oppressive any longer. Martin Beck found no reason to overtax his strength. He strolled slowly along the paths in the spacious park, often stopping to look around. He saw no sign of his shadow. Perhaps they had at last realized how harmless he was and had given up. On the other hand, the whole island was swarming with people and it was difficult to pick out anyone special in the crowd, especially when one had no idea what the person concerned looked like. He made his way down to the water on the eastern side of the island and followed the shoreline out to a landing stage where all the boats he had previously ridden on came in. He thought he could even remember the name of the station: Casino.

Along the edge of the shore above the landing stage stood a row of benches where a few people were waiting for the boats. On one of them sat one of the few people in Budapest familiar to him: the easily frightened girl from the house in Újpest. Ari Boeck was wearing sunglasses, sandals and a white dress with shoulder straps. She was reading a German paperback and beside her on the bench lay a nylon string bag. His first thought was to walk past, but then he regretted it, halted and said, "Good afternoon."

She raised her eyes and looked at him blankly. Then she appeared to recognize him and smiled.

"Oh, it's you, is it? Have you found your friend?"

"No, not yet."

"I thought about it after you'd gone yesterday. I can't understand how he came to give you my address."

"I don't understand it either."

"I thought about it last night too," she said frowning. "I could hardly sleep."

"Yes, it's peculiar."

(Not at all, my dear girl, there's an extremely simple explanation. For one thing, he didn't give me any address. For another, this is probably what happened: he saw you in Stockholm when you were swimming and thought there's a sweet piece, I'd like to—yes, exactly. And then when he came here six months later, he found out your address and the location of your street, but didn't have time to go there.)

"Won't you sit down? It's almost too hot to be standing upright today."

He sat down as she moved the nylon net. It held two things he recognized, namely the dark-blue bathing suit and the green rubber mask, as well as a rolled-up bath towel and a bottle of suntan oil.

(Martin Beck, the born detective and famous observer, constantly occupied making useless observations and storing them away for future use. Doesn't even have bats in his belfry —they couldn't get in for all the crap in the way.)

"Are you waiting for the boat too?"

"Yes," he said. "But we're probably going in different directions."

"I don't have anything special to do. I was thinking of going home, of course."

"Have you been swimming?"

(The art of deduction.)

"Yes, of course. Why do you ask that?"

(Well, that's a very good question.)

"What have you done with your boyfriend today?"

(What the hell has that got to do with me? Oh, it's just an interrogation technique.)

"Tetz? He's gone. Anyway, he's not my boyfriend."

"Oh, isn't he?"

(Extremely spiritual.)

"Just a boy I know. He stays at the boarding house now and again. He's a nice guy."

She shrugged her shoulders. He looked at her feet. They were still short and broad with straight toes.

(Martin Beck, the incorruptible, more interested in a woman's shoe size than the color of her nipples.)

"Uh-huh. And now you're going home, are you?"

(The wearing-them-down treatment.)

"Well, I thought I would. I don't have anything special to do around this time of the summer. What are you going to do yourself?"

"I don't know."

(At last a word of truth.)

"Have you been up to Gellért Hill to look at the view? From the Liberation Memorial?"

"No."

"You can see the whole city from there, as if it were on a tray."

"Mm-m."

"Shall we go there? Perhaps there'll even be a little breeze up there."

"Why not?" said Martin Beck.

(You can always keep your eyes open.)

"Then we'll take the boat that's coming in now. You would have taken that one anyway."

The boat was called Ifjugárda and had probably been built on the same design as the steamer he had been on the day before. The ventilators, however, were constructed differently and the funnel was slightly aft-braced.

They stood by the railing. The boat slid swiftly midstream toward Margaret Bridge. Just under the arch, she said, "What's your name, by the way."

"Martin."

"Mine's Ari. But you knew that before, didn't you—however that happened."

He gave no reply to that, but after a while said, "What does this name mean—Ifjugárda?"

"A member of the Youth Guard."

The view from the Liberation Memorial lived up to her promise and more so. There was even a little breeze up there, too. They had gone all the way on the boat to the last stop in front of the famous Gellért Hotel, then walked a bit along a street named after Béla Bártok and finally got on a bus which slowly and laboriously had taken them to the top of the hill.

Now they were standing on the parapet of the citadel above the monument. Beneath them lay the city, with hundreds of thousands of windows glowing in the late afternoon sun. They were standing so close to each other that he felt a light, brushing touch when she swung her body. For the first time in five days, he allowed himself to be caught thinking about something other than Alf Matsson.

"There's the museum I work in, over there," she said. "It's closed during the summer."

"Oh."

"Otherwise I go to the university."

"Uh-huh."

They went down on foot, along twisting paths traversing the bank down to the river. Then they walked across the new bridge and found themselves close to his hotel. The sun had rolled down below the hills in the northwest and a soft, warm dusk had fallen over the river.

"Well, what shall we do now?" said Ari Boeck.

She held him lightly by his arm and swung her body playfully as they walked along the quay.

"We could talk about Alf Matsson," said Martin Beck.

The woman gave him a swift look of reproach, but the next moment was smiling as she said, "Yes, why not? How is he? Are you great friends?"

"No, not at all. I only . . . know him."

At this stage he was almost convinced that she was telling the truth and that his vague idea that had taken him to the house in Újpest had been a false trail. But it's an ill wind that brings no one any good, he thought.

She was clinging to his arm a little now and zigzagging with her feet so that her body swung back and forth on a vertical axle.

"What kind of boat is that?" he said.

"It goes on moonlight cruises up the river, then around Margaret Island and back. It takes about an hour. Costs next to nothing. Shall we go along on it?"

They went on board and soon afterward the boat set out, peacefully splashing in the dark current. Of all the types of engine-driven vessels yet constructed, there is none that moves so pleasantly as the paddle steamer.

They stood above the wheelhouse and watched the shores gliding by. She leaned against him, quite lightly, and he now felt very clearly something he had noticed earlier: that she had no bra on under her dress.

A small ensemble was playing on the afterdeck and a number of people were dancing.

"Do you want to dance?" she said.

"No," said Martin Beck.

"Good. I don't think it's much fun either."

A moment later she said, "But I can, if necessary."

"So can I," said Martin Beck.

The boat passed Margaret Island and Újpest, before turning and soundlessly gliding back southward with the current. They stood behind the funnel for a moment and looked through the open hatches. The engine was beating with calm pulse beats, the copper pipes were shining and the warm oily current of air was flung upward in their direction.

"Have you been on this boat before?" he said.

"Yes, many a time. It's the best thing to do in this city on a really hot evening."

He did not really know who she was and what he thought of her, and this, above all else, irritated him.

The boat passed the colossal Parliament building—where nowadays a small red star shone discreetly above the central cupola—and then it slipped its lowered funnel under the bridge with large stone lions on it and hove to at the same place as where they started.

As they walked along the gangplank, Martin Beck let his eyes sweep over the quay. Under the lamp by the ticket office stood the tall man with dark hair brushed back on his head. He was again wearing his blue suit and was staring straight at them. A moment later the man turned around and vanished with swift steps behind the shelter. The woman followed Martin Beck's glance and put her left hand in his right one, suddenly but carefully.

"Did you see that man?" he said.

"Yes," she said.

"Do you know who he is?"

She shook her head.

"No. Do you?"

"No, not yet."

Martin Beck felt hungry for once. He had had no lunch and the dinner hour would soon be over.

"Would you like to come and have a meal with me?"

"Where?"

"At the hotel."

"Can I go there in these clothes?"

"Sure."

He almost added, "We're not in Sweden now."

Quite a number of people were still in the dining room and along the balustrade outside the open windows. Swarms of insects were dancing around the lamps.

"Little gnats," she said. "They don't sting. When they disappear, the summer's over. Did you know that?"

The food was excellent, as usual, and so was the wine. She was evidently hungry and ate with a healthy, youthful greed. Then she sat still and listened to the music. They smoked with their coffee and drank a kind of cherry-brandy liqueur which also tasted of chocolate. When she put out her cigarette in the ash tray, she brushed his right hand with her fingertips, as if by accident. A little later she repeated the maneuver and soon after that he felt her foot against his ankle under the table. Evidently she had kicked off her sandal.

After a while she moved her foot and her hand away and went off to the powder room.

Martin Beck thoughtfully massaged his hairline with the fingers of his right hand. Then he leaned over the table and picked up the nylon string bag that was lying on the chair beside him. He thrust his hand into it, unfolded the bathing suit and felt it. The material was completely dry, even in the seams and along the elastic. So dry that it could hardly have been in contact with water during the past twenty-four hours. He rolled up the bathing suit, put the net carefully back on the chair and bit his knuckle thoughtfully. Naturally it did not necessarily mean anything. In any case, he was still behaving like an idiot.

She came back and sat down, smiling at him. She crossed her legs, lit another cigarette and listened to the Viennese melody.

"How lovely it is," she said.

He nodded.

The dining room began to empty, the waiters gathering together in groups, talking. The musicians ended the evening's concert with "The Blue Danube." She looked at the clock.

"I must be going home."

He thought about this intensely. One floor up there was a small night-club-type bar with jazz music, but he loathed that kind of place so profoundly that only the most pressing assignment could make him go into them. Perhaps this was just what this was?

"How will you get home?" he said. "By boat?"

"No, the last one's gone. I'll go by trolley. It's quicker, in fact."

He went on thinking. In all its simplicity, the situation was somewhat complicated. Why, he did not know.

He chose to do nothing and say nothing. The musicians went away, bowing in exhaustion. She looked at the clock again.

"I'd better go now," she said.

The night porter bowed in the vestibule. The doorman whirled them respectfully out through the revolving doors.

They stood on the pavement, alone in the warm night air. She took a short step so that she was standing facing him, with her right leg between his. She stood on tiptoe and kissed him. Very clearly, he felt her breasts and stomach and loins and thighs through the material of her dress. She could hardly reach up to him.

"Oh my, how tall you are," she said.

She made a small supple movement and again stood firmly on the ground, an inch or so from him.

"Thank you for everything," she said. "See you again soon. Bye."

She walked away, turned her head and waved her right hand. The net with her bathing things in it swung against her left leg.

"Bye," said Martin Beck.

He went back into the vestibule, picked up his key and went up to his room. It was stuffy in there and he opened the window at once. He took off his shirt and shoes, went out to the bathroom and rinsed his face and chest with cold water. He felt a bigger idiot than ever.

"I must be completely nuts," he said. "What luck no one saw me."

At that moment there was a light tap on the door. The handle went down, and she came in.

"I crept past," she said. "No one saw me."

She closed the door behind her, quickly and quietly, took two steps into the room, dropped the net onto the floor and stepped out of her sandals. He stared at her. Her eyes had changed and were cloudy, as if there were a veil over them. She bent down with her arms crossed, took hold of the hem of her dress with both hands and pulled off her dress in one swift movement. She had nothing on underneath. This in itself was not so surprising. Obviously she always sunbathed in the same bathing suit, for across her breasts and hips ran sharply demarcated areas which looked chalk-white against the rest of her dark-brown skin. Her breasts were smooth and white and round, and her nipples were large and pink and cylindrical, like anchored buoys. The jet-black hair growing up from her loins was also sharply demarcated: an inscribed triangle that filled a considerable part of the rectangular, white strip of skin. The hair was curly and thick and stiff, as if electric. The areas around her nipples was circular and light-brown. She looked like a highly colored geometrical old man.

His depressing years with the Public Morals Squad had made Martin Beck immune to provocations of this kind. And even if this were perhaps not really provocation in the proper sense of the term, he still found the situation far easier to deal with than what had irritated him in the dining room half an hour earlier. Before she even had time to get her dress over her head, he put his hand on her shoulder and said:

"Just a minute."

She lowered the dress a little and looked at him over the hem with glazed brown eyes, which neither reacted nor comprehended. She had got her left arm free from the dress. She stretched it out, gripped hold of his right hand and slowly drew it down between her legs. Her sex was swollen and open. Vaginal secretion ran down his fingers.

"Feel it," she said, with a sort of helplessness, far beyond good or evil.

Martin Beck freed himself, stretched out his arm, opened the door to the hotel corridor and said in his schoolroom German:

"Please dress yourself."

She stood still for a moment, quite nonplussed, just as when he had knocked on the door in Újpest. Then she obeyed.

He put on his shirt and shoes, picked up her string bag and led her down to the vestibule with a light grip on her arm.

"Call for a taxi," he said to the night porter.

The taxi came almost at once. He opened the door, but as he was going to help her in, she freed herself vehemently.

"I'll pay the driver," he said.

She cast a look at him. The cloudy veil had gone. The patient had recovered. Her eyes were clear and dark and full of loathing.

"Like hell you will," she said. "Drive on."

She slammed the door and the taxi rolled away.

Martin Beck looked around. It was already long past midnight. He walked a bit south, up onto the new bridge, which was also deserted except for a few night trolleys. He stopped in the middle of the bridge and leaned against the railing, looking down into the silently running water. It was warm and empty and silent. An ideal place to think—if a man only knew what to think. After a while he went back to the hotel. Ari Boeck had dropped a cigarette with a red filter tip on the floor. He picked it up and lit it. It tasted unpleasant and he threw it out the window.

15

Martin Beck was lying in the bathtub when the telephone rang.

He had slept past breakfast and taken a walk on the quay before lunch. The sun was hotter than ever, and even down by the river, the air was not moving at all. When he returned to the hotel, he had felt a greater need for a quick bath than for food, and had decided to let lunch wait. Now he was lying in the lukewarm water and heard the telephone ring with short quick signals.

He climbed out of the tub, swept a large bath towel around him and lifted the receiver.

"Mr. Beck?"

"Yes?"

"Please forgive me for not using your title. As you will understand, it is purely—well, let's say a, well . . . precautionary measure."

It was the young man from the Embassy. Martin Beck wondered whom this precautionary measure was against, as both the hotel people and Szluka knew he was a policeman, but he said, "Of course."

"How are things going? Have you made any progress?"

Martin Beck let the bath towel fall and sat down on the bed. "No," he said.

"Haven't you got any clues?"

"No," said Martin Beck.

There was a brief silence, and then he added, "I've spoken to the police here."

"I think that was a singularly unwise move," said the man from the Embassy.

"Possibly," said Martin Beck. "I could hardly avoid it. I was visited by a gentleman called Vilmos Szluka."

"Major Szluka. What did he want?"

"Nothing. He probably said more or less the same thing to me as he already said to you. That he had no reason to take up the case."

"I see. What are you thinking of doing now?"

"Having some lunch," said Martin Beck.

"I mean about the matter we were discussing."

"I don't know."

There was another silence. Then the young man said, "Well, you know where to phone if there's anything."

"Yes."

"Good-bye, then."

"Good-bye."

Martin Beck put down the receiver and went out and pulled the plug out of the bathtub. Then he dressed and went down and sat under the awning outside the dining room and ordered lunch.

It was uncomfortably hot even in the shade of the awning.

He ate slowly, taking large gulps of the cold beer. He had an unpleasant feeling of being watched. He had not seen the tall, dark-haired man, but all the same he continually felt he was under surveillance.

He looked at the people around him. They were the usual gathering of lunch guests—mostly foreigners like himself and most of them staying at the hotel. He heard scattered fragments of conversation, mainly in German and Hungarian, but also English and some language he could not identify.

Suddenly he heard someone behind him say quite clearly in Swedish: "Crispbread." He turned around and saw two ladies, undeniably Swedish, sitting by the window in the dining room.

He heard one of them say, "Yes, I always take some with me. And toilet paper. It's always so bad abroad. If there is any at all."

"Yes," said the other. "I remember once in Spain . . ."

Martin Beck gave up listening to this typically Swedish conversation, and devoted himself to trying to decide which of those sitting around him was his shadow. For a long time he suspected a man who was past middle age—he was sitting some way away with his back to him and kept glancing over his shoulder in his direction. But then the man got up and lifted down a fluffy little dog that had been sitting, concealed, on his lap and vanished with the dog around the corner of the hotel.

When Martin Beck had finished eating and had drunk a cup of that strong coffee, much of the afternoon was already gone. It was exhaustingly hot, but he walked up into town for a bit, trying to keep in the shade all the time. He had discovered that the police station was only a few blocks away from the hotel and had no difficulty in finding it. On the steps—where the key had been found, according to Szluka—there was a patrolman in blue-gray uniform standing wiping the sweat from his forehead.

Martin Beck circled the police station and took another route home, all the time with an unpleasant feeling he was being watched. This was something quite new to him. During his twenty-three years with the police, he had many times been involved in keeping a watch on suspected persons and shadowing them. Only now did he understand to the full what it felt like to be shadowed. To know that all the while one was being observed and watched, that every movement one made was being registered, that all the time someone was keeping himself hidden somewhere in the vicinity, following every step one took.

Martin Beck went up to his room and stayed there in the relative cool for the rest of the day. He sat at the table with a piece of paper in front of him and a pen in hand, trying to make some kind of summary of what he knew about the Alf Matsson case.

In the end he tore up the paper into little pieces and flushed them down the toilet. What he knew was so infinitesimal that it seemed simply foolish to write it down. He would not have to strain himself to keep it all in mind. Actually, thought Martin Beck, he knew no more than what could be contained in a shrimp's brain.

The sun went down and colored the river red, the brief dusk passed unnoticeably into a velvet darkness, and with the dark came the first cool breezes from the hills down across the river.

Martin Beck stood by his window and watched the surface of the water being rippled by the light evening breeze. A man was standing by a tree just below his window. A cigarette glowed and Martin Beck thought he recognized the tall dark man. In some way it was a relief to see him there, to escape that vague, creeping sense of his presence in the vicinity.

He put on a suit, went down to the dining room and had dinner. He ate as slowly as possible and drank two *barack palinkas* before going up to his room again.

The evening breeze had gone, the river lay black and shiny, and the heat was just as suffocating outside as inside in the room.

Martin Beck left the windows and shutters open and drew back the curtains. Then he undressed and got into the creaking bed.

16

Heat that is really intense almost always becomes harder to tolerate when the sun has gone down. Anyone who is used to heat knows the routine and closes the window and shutters and draws the curtains. Like most Scandinavians, Martin Beck lacked these instincts. He had drawn back the curtains and opened the windows wide and was lying on his back in the dark, waiting for the cool air. It never came. He switched on the bedside lamp and tried to read. That did not work very well either. He did have a box of sleeping tablets in the bathroom, but was not very willing to take that way out. The past day had gone by without any positive achievements on his part and consequently there was every reason for him to try to remain on the alert and somehow produce results tomorrow. If he took the sleeping tablets, he would be walking around as if in a trance the next morning: he knew this of old.

He got up and sat down by the open window. The difference was infinitesimal: there was not the slightest draft, nor even a hot breeze from the Hungarian steppes, wherever they were. The city seemed almost as if it, too, had difficulty breathing, had fallen into a coma and become unconscious from the heat. After a while a lone yellow trolley appeared on the other side of the river. It drove slowly across Elisabeth Bridge, and the sound of the wheels' friction against the rails echoed and grew louder under the arch of the bridge before it rolled away across the water. Despite the distance, he could see that it was empty. Twenty-three hours earlier, he had been standing up there on the bridge, puzzling over his strange meeting with the woman from Újpest. It had not been a bad place.

He pulled on his trousers and shirt and went out. The porter's desk was empty. On the street, a green Skoda started up and drove slowly and reluctantly around the corner. Pairs of lovers in cars are the same the world over. He walked along the edge of the quay—past some sleeping boats—went by the statue of the Hungarian poet Petőfi and then came up onto the bridge. It was quite silent and deserted, as on the preceding night, and was clearly lit up, in contrast to many of the city streets. Again he stopped on the middle of the bridge, his elbows on the parapet, and stared down into the water. A tugboat passed beneath him. Far behind it came its load, four long barges tied together in pairs. Soundlessly gliding with all their lights extinguished, only a shade darker than the night.

As he moved on a few yards, he heard his own footsteps give a faint echo somewhere on the silent bridge. He walked on a bit farther and again heard the echo. It seemed as if the sound could be heard a trifle too long. He stood still listening for a long time, but heard nothing. Then he walked quickly on for about twenty yards and stopped suddenly. The sound came again, and this time, too, he thought it came too late to be truly an echo. He walked as quietly as he could across to the other side of the bridge and looked back. It was quite silent now. Nothing moved. A trolley from the Pest side came up onto the bridge and made any further observations impossible. Martin Beck continued his promenade across the bridge. Evidently he was suffering from persecution mania. If someone had the energy and resources to watch him at this time of night, then it could hardly be anyone else but the police. And with that the problem was largely solved. So long as . . .

Martin Beck was almost over the bridge below Gellért Hill when the trolley rattled past. A lone passenger was sleeping with his mouth open, leaning against one of the windows.

He reached the steps leading down to the quay from the south side of the bridge and began to walk down them.

Through the retreating rattle of the trolley, he thought he heard the sound of a car, which stopped somewhere in the vicinity, but he could not decide how far away or in which direction from him.

Martin Beck had reached the quay. Swiftly and silently he walked south, away from the bridge, and stopped where the darkness was thickest. He turned around, stood quite still and listened. Nothing could be heard or seen. In all probability there was no one on the bridge, but this in itself was not certain. If someone had followed him from the other side, he could easily also have got to the end of the bridge and gone down to the quay from the north side of the bridge. He was sure that no one other than himself had gone down the south steps.

The slight sounds which could be heard now came from traffic very far away. There was complete silence in the immediate vicinity. Martin Beck smiled in the darkness. He was now almost convinced that no one had followed him, but the game amused him, and in his innermost self he wished that there were some confused fellow creature over there in the dark on the other side of the bridge. He himself knew the routine backward and forward and knew that whoever might have gone down on the other side could not take the risk of returning the same way, crossing the bridge and going down the steps on the south side. Under the bridge two parallel streets ran along the quay, the inner one nearly six feet higher than the quay itself, which in its turn sloped down toward the river in steps. The two streets were separated by a low wall. Farther up, there was also a tunnel through the actual foundations of the bridge. But none of these ways was accessible to anyone shadowing him, provided that person knew his job. Every attempt to pass under the bridge would mean that the man would have the light behind him and thus risk immediate discovery. Consequently only one alternative remained: to go around the entire abutment of the bridge in a wide semicircle, cross several approach ramps and make his way down onto the quay as far south as possible. But this would take some time, even if the man took the risk of running, and during that time the person being shadowed—in this case Inspector Martin Beck from Stockholm—would have time to vanish in practically any direction he chose.

Now it was unlikely, however, that there was anyone shadowing him at all, and in addition Martin Beck had intended to walk north along the river and return to the hotel via the next bridge. Consequently, he left his observation post in the sheltering darkness and walked north at an easy pace. He chose the inner of the two streets, passed under the bridge and continued along the stone wall, six feet above the quay. On the opposite shore the hotel was dark except for two narrow perpendicular rectangles of light. The windows of his own room. He sat down on the low stone wall and lit a cigarette. Large houses of the kind built at the turn of the century lined the street. In front of them stood parked cars. All the windows were shuttered and dark. Martin Beck sat still and listened to the silence. He was still on guard, but without being conscious of the fact himself.

On the other side of the street a car engine started up. He let his eyes sweep along the row of parked vehicles but could not locate the noise. The engine was turning over slowly, purring. This continued for about thirty seconds. Then he heard the car being put into gear. A pair of parking lights went on. More than fifty yards ahead a car came out of the shadows and moved away from the edge of the pavement. It came in his direction, but on the other side of the street, and extremely slowly. A dark-green Skoda, and he had a feeling he had seen it before. The car came nearer. Martin Beck sat still on the stone wall and followed it with his eyes. Almost level with him, it began to turn to the left, as if the driver were going to turn around in the street. But the turn was not completed: the car was moving almost more slowly than before, straight at him. Obviously someone wanted to meet him, but his way of going about it was astounding. The idea could hardly be to run him down—not at that speed—and, besides, he could get to safety behind the wall in a second, if necessary. Provided no one was hiding in the back seat, there was only one person in the car.

Martin Beck put out his cigarette. He was in no way afraid, but very curious to know what was going to happen.

The green Skoda had stopped with its engine running and its right front wheel against the curb, only nine feet away from him. The driver switched on the headlights and everything was drowned in a flood of light. But only for a few seconds, then all the lights went out. The car door opened and a man stepped out onto the pavement.

Martin Beck had seen him often enough to be able to recognize him at once, despite the blinding effect of the light. The tall man with dark hair brushed back on his head. The man was empty-handed. He took a step nearer. The engine of the car purred slowly.

He sensed something. Not a shadow, nor even a sound, only a small movement in the air, just behind him. So faint that only the stillness of the night made it perceptible.

Martin Beck knew that he was no longer alone on the wall, that the car was only meant to distract his attention while someone silently approached down on the quay and heaved himself up onto the stone wall behind him.

And in the same second he also realized clearly and penetratingly that this was not shadowing, not a game, but deadly serious. And more than that. It was death: this time out for *him*, and not by chance, but in a cold, calculated, premeditated fashion.

Martin Beck was a bad fighter, but his reflex actions were remarkable. At the exact moment he felt the slight draft, he ducked his head down between his shoulders, put his right foot upon the edge of the wall, kicked away, twisted his body and threw himself backward, all in one lightning movement. The arm that had been on its way around his throat was pressed hard against the ridge of his nose and eyebrows before it slid away over his forehead. He felt a hot, astonished breath against his cheek and caught the swift glint of a knife blade, which had already missed its mark and was on its way away from him. He fell backward down onto the quay, hit his left shoulder hard on the stone paving and rolled around to give himself time, if possible, to get his balance and get onto his feet. On the wall he saw two figures, silhouetted against the starry sky. Then there was only one and while he still had one knee on the stone paving, the man with the knife was on him again. His left arm was temporarily paralyzed after his fall against the quay, but for a second or two the light was in his favor: he himself was low in the dark and the other man was etched against the background. His attacker missed and a second later Martin Beck managed to seize hold of the man's right wrist. It was not a good grip and the wrist was unusually large, but he held on, very conscious of the fact that it was his only chance. For a tenth of a second or so, they stood up and he noted that the other man was shorter than himself, but considerably broader. Mechanically, he applied one of the hoary old method holds learned at police college and succeeded in getting his opponent onto the ground. The only thing wrong was that he did not dare let go of the hand with the knife and was himself drawn down in the fall. They rolled around once and were now extremely close to the edge of the quay, where the steps down to the water began. The paralysis in his left arm had let up and he got a hold on the man's other wrist. But his opponent was stronger and slowly broke away. A hard kick in the head reminded him that he was not only physically but also numerically inferior. He was now lying on his back so close to the stairs that he felt the first step with his foot. The man with the knife was panting heavily in his face, smelling of sweat, shaving water and throat pastilles. His opponent began slowly but relentlessly to free his right hand.

Martin Beck felt it was all over—at least very nearly. Lightning bolts clashed in the throbbing haze, his heart seemed to swell more and more and more, like a purple tumor about to burst. His head was thumping like a pile driver. He thought he heard terrible roars, shots, piercing shrieks, and he saw the world drowned in a flood of blinding white light that obliterated all shapes and all life. His last conscious thought was that he was going to die here on a quay in a foreign city, just as Alf Matsson had presumably done, and without knowing why.

With a last reflex-like effort, Martin Beck gripped the other man's right wrist with both hands as he kicked with his foot and tipped both himself and his opponent over the edge of the quay. He hit his head on the second step and lost consciousness.

Martin Beck opened his eyes after an epoch of time that seemed boundless, and that in any case must have been very long. Everything was bathed in a white light. He was lying on his back with his head to one side and his right ear against the stone paving. The first thing he saw was a pair of well-polished black shoes, which almost filled his field of vision. He turned his head and looked up.

Szluka, in a gray suit and with that silly hunting hat still on his head, bent down over him and said:

"Good evening."

Martin Beck propped himself up on his elbow. The flood of light was coming from two police cars, one on the quay and the other driven up to the stone wall on the street above. About ten feet away from Szluka stood a policeman in a visored cap, black leather boots and a light-gray-blue uniform. He was holding a black night stick in his right hand and looking thoughtfully at a person lying at his feet. It was Tetz Radeberger, the man who had played with Ari Boeck's bathing suit in the house in Újpest. He was now on his back, deeply unconscious, with blood on his forehead and in his blond hair.

"The other one," said Martin Beck. "Where is he?"

"Shot," said Szluka. "Carefully, of course. In the leg."

A number of windows had been thrown open in the houses along the street and people were peering inquisitively down toward the quay.

"Lie still," said Szluka. "The ambulance will be here soon."

"No need," said Martin Beck, beginning to get up.

Exactly three minutes and fifteen seconds had passed since he had been sitting on the stone wall and had felt that draft at the back of his neck.

17

The car was a blue-and-white 1962 model Warsvawa. It had a flashing blue light on the roof and the siren sounded in a subdued, melancholy wail along the empty night streets. The word RENDŐRSÉG was painted in block capitals in the white band across the front door. It meant police.

Martin Beck was sitting in the back seat. At his side sat a uniformed officer. Szluka was sitting in the front seat, to the right of the driver.

"You did well," said Szluka. "Rather dangerous young men, those two."

"Who put Radeberger out of action?"

"He's sitting beside you," said Szluka. Martin Beck turned his head. The policeman had a narrow black mustache and brown eyes with a sympathetic look in them.

"He speaks only Hungarian," said Szluka.

"What's his name?"

"Foti."

Martin Beck put out his hand.

"Thanks, Foti," he said.

"He had to give it to them pretty hard," said Szluka. "Hadn't much time."

"Lucky he was around," said Martin Beck.

"We're usually around," said Szluka. "Except in the cartoons."

"They have their hangout in Újpest," said Martin Beck. "A boarding house on Venetianer út."

"We know that."

Szluka sat quietly a moment. Then he asked, "How did you come into contact with them?"

"Through a woman named Boeck. Matsson had asked for her address. And she had been in Stockholm. Competing as a swimmer. There could be a connection. That's why I looked her up."

"And what did she say?"

"That she was studying at the university and working at a museum. And that she had never heard of Matsson."

They had reached the police station at Deák Ferenc Tér. The car swung into a concrete yard and stopped. Martin Beck followed Szluka up to his office. It was very spacious and the wall was covered with a large map of Budapest, but to all intents and purposes it reminded him of his own office back in Stockholm. Szluka hung up his hunting hat and pointed to a chair. He opened his mouth, but before he had time to say anything, the telephone rang. He went over to his desk and answered. Martin Beck thought he could make out a torrent of words. It went on for a long time. Now and again Szluka replied in monosyllables. After a while he looked at his watch, exploded in a rapid, irritated harangue and put down the receiver.

"My wife," he said.

He went over to the map and studied the northern part of the city, with his back to his visitor.

"Being a policeman," said Szluka, "is not a profession. And it's certainly not a vocation either. It's a curse."

A little later he turned around and said:

"Of course, I don't mean that. Only think it sometimes. Are you married?"

"Yes."

"Then you know."

A policeman in uniform came in and put down a tray with

two cups of coffee on it. They drank. Szluka looked at his watch.

"We're searching the place up there at the moment. The report should soon be here."

"How did you manage to be around?" said Martin Beck.

Szluka replied with exactly the same sentence as in the car.

"We're usually around."

Then he smiled and said, "It was what you said about being shadowed. Naturally it wasn't us watching you. Why should we do that?"

Martin Beck poked his nose, a little conscience-stricken.

"People imagine so many things," said Szluka. "But of course you're a policeman, and policemen seldom do. So we began to watch the man who was tailing you. Backtailing as the Americans call it, if I remember rightly. This afternoon our man saw that there were two men watching you. He thought it looked peculiar and sounded the alarm. It's as simple as that."

Martin Beck nodded. Szluka looked at him thoughtfully.

"And yet it was all so quick we just barely got there in time."

He finished his coffee and carefully put his cup down.

"Backtailing," he said, as if savoring the word. "Have you ever been to America?"

"No."

"Neither have I."

"I worked with them on a case, two years ago. With someone called Kafka."

"Sounds Czech."

"It was an American tourist who got murdered in Sweden. Ugly story. Complicated investigation."

Szluka sat silent for a moment. Then he said abruptly, "How did it go?"

"O.K.," said Martin Beck.

"I've only read about the American police. They have a peculiar organization. Difficult to understand."

Martin Beck nodded.

"And a lot to do," said Szluka. "They have as many murders in New York in a week as we have in the whole country in a year."

A uniformed police officer with two stars on his shoulder straps came into the room. He discussed something with Szluka, saluted Martin Beck and left. While the door was standing open, Ari Boeck walked along the corridor outside, with a woman guard. She was wearing the same white dress and the same sandals as the day before, but had a shawl over her shoulders. She threw a flat, vacant look at Martin Beck.

"Nothing of importance in Újpest," said Szluka. "We're taking the car apart now. When Radeberger comes around and the other one has been patched up, we'll tackle them. There's quite a bit I still don't understand."

He fell silent, hesitantly.

"But things will clear up soon."

The telephone rang and he was occupied for a while. Martin Beck understood nothing of the conversation except now and again the word *"Svéd"* and *"Svédország"* which he knew meant Swede or Swedish and Sweden. Szluka put down the receiver and said, "This must have something to do with your compatriot, Matsson."

"Yes, of course."

"The girl lied to you, by the way. She's not studied at the university and doesn't work at a museum. She doesn't really seem to do anything. Got suspended from competitive swimming because she didn't behave herself."

"There must be some connection."

"Yes, but where? Oh well, we'll see."

Szluka shrugged his shoulders. Martin Beck turned and twisted his mangled body. It ached in his shoulders and arms, and his head was far from what it ought to be. He felt very tired and found it difficult to think, and yet did not want to go home to bed at the hotel, all the same.

The telephone rang again. Szluka listened with a frown, and then his eyes cleared.

"Things are beginning to move," he said. "We've found

something. And one of them is all right now, the tall one. His name's Fröbe, by the way. Now we'll see. Are you coming along?"

Martin Beck began to get up.

"Or perhaps you'd rather rest for a while."

"No, thank you," said Martin Beck.

18

Szluka sat down behind the desk with his hands clasped loosely in front of him, a passport with a green cover at his right elbow.

The tall man in the chair opposite Szluka had dark shadows under his eyes. Martin Beck knew that he had not had much sleep during the last twenty-four hours. The man was sitting up straight in the chair, looking down at his hands.

Szluka nodded at the stenographer and began.

The man raised his eyes and looked at Szluka.

"Your name?"

"Theodor Fröbe."

SZLUKA: When were you born?

FRÖBE: Twenty-first of April, 1936, in Hanover.

SZ: And you are a West German citizen. Living where?

F: In Hamburg. Hermannstrasse 12.

SZ: What is your occupation?

F: Travel guide. Or to be more correct, travel-agency official.

SZ: Where are you employed?

F: At a travel agency called Winkler's.

SZ: Where do you live in Budapest?

F: At a boarding house in Újpest. Venetianer út 6.

SZ: And why are you in Budapest?

F: I represent the travel agency and look after parties traveling to and from Budapest.

SZ: Earlier tonight you and a man called Tetz Radeberger

were caught in the act of attacking a man on Groza Peter Rak-part. You were both armed and your intention to injure or kill the man was obvious. Do you know this man?

F: No.

sz: Have you seen him before?

F: . . .

sz: Answer me!

F: No.

sz: Do you know who he is?

F: No.

sz: You don't know him, you've never seen him before and don't know who he is. Why did you attack him?

F: . . . . .

sz: Explain why you attacked him!

F: We . . . needed money and . . .

sz: And?

F: And then we saw him down there on the quay and—

sz: You're lying. Please don't lie to me. It's no good. The attack was planned and you were armed. In addition, it is a lie that you've not seen him before. You have been following him for two days. Why? Answer me!

F: We thought he was someone else.

sz: That he was who?

F: Someone who . . . who . . .

sz: Who?

F: Who owed us money.

sz: And so you followed him and attacked him?

F: Yes.

sz: I've already warned you once. It is extremely unwise of you to lie. I know exactly when you are lying. Do you know a Swede called Alf Matsson?

F: No.

sz: Your friends Radeberger and Boeck have already said that you know him.

F: I know him only slightly. I didn't remember that that was his name.

sz: When did you last see Alf Matsson?

F: In May, I think it was.

sz: Where did you meet him?

F: Here in Budapest.

sz: And you haven't seen him since then?

F: No.

sz: Three days ago this man was at your boarding house asking for Alf Matsson. Since then you have followed him and tonight you tried to kill him. Why?

F: Not kill him!

sz: Why?

F: We didn't try to kill him!

sz: But you attacked him, didn't you? And you were armed with a knife.

F: Yes, but it was a mistake. Nothing happened to him, did it? He wasn't injured, was he? You've no right to question me like this.

sz: How long have you known Alf Matsson?

F: About a year. I don't remember exactly.

sz: How did you meet?

F: At a mutual friend's place here in Budapest.

sz: What's your friend's name?

F: Ari Boeck.

sz: Have you met him several times since then?

F: A few times. Not very many.

sz: Did you always meet here in Budapest?

F: We've met in Prague too. And in Warsaw.

sz: And in Bratislava.

F: Yes.

sz: And in Constanta?

F: . . . . .

sz: Didn't you?

F: Yes.

sz: How did it happen? That you met in all those cities where none of you lived?

F: I travel a lot. It's my job. And he traveled a lot too. It turned out that we met there.

sz: Why did you meet?

F: We just met. We were good friends.

sz: Now you are saying that you've been meeting him over a year in at least five different cities because you are good friends. A moment ago you were saying that you knew him only slightly. Why didn't you want to admit that you knew him?

F: I was nervous from sitting here being questioned. And I'm awfully tired. And my leg hurts, too.

sz: Oh yes. So you're very tired. Was Tetz Radeberger also with you when you met Alf Matsson at all these different places?

F: Yes, we work for the same agency and travel together.

sz: How did it happen, do you think, that Radeberger didn't want to admit at once to knowing Alf Matsson either? Was he awfully tired, too, perhaps?

F: I don't know anything about that.

sz: Do you know where Alf Matsson is right now?

F: No, I have no idea.

sz: Do you want me to tell you?

F: Yes.

sz: I'm not going to do it, however. How long have you been employed at this Winkler's travel agency?

F: For six years.

sz: Is it a well-paid job?

F: Not especially. But I get everything free when I'm traveling. Food, keep and fares.

sz: But the salary isn't high?

F: No. But I manage.

sz: It seems so. You have enough so that you manage.

F: What do you mean by that?

sz: You have in fact fifteen hundred dollars, eight hundred and thirty pounds and ten thousand marks. That's a lot of money. Where did you get it from?

F: That's nothing to do with you.

sz: Answer my question and don't use that tone of voice.

F: It's not your business where I get my money from.

sz: It's possible and also very likely that you haven't half the sense I thought you had, but even with the very slightest intelligence, you ought to be able to see that you would be wiser to answer my questions. Well, where did you get the money from?

F: I did extra jobs and earned it all over a long period.

sz: What sort of jobs?

F: Different things.

Szluka looked at Fröbe and opened a drawer in his desk. Out of the drawer he took a package wrapped up in plastic. The package was about eight inches long and four inches wide and fastened with adhesive tape. Szluka put the package down on the desk between himself and Fröbe. All the while he was looking at Fröbe, whose eyes wavered, trying to avoid looking at the package. Szluka looked straight at him and Fröbe wiped away the sweat that had appeared in little beads around his nose. Then Szluka added, "Uh-huh. Different things. As for example, smuggling and selling hashish. A profitable occupation, but not in the long run, Herr Fröbe."

F: I don't understand what you're talking about.

sz: No? And you don't recognize this little package either?

F: No, I don't. Why should I?

sz: And not the fifteen similar packages that were found hidden in the doors and upholstery of Radeberger's car, either?

F: .....

sz: There's quite a lot of hashish in just one little package like this. We're not accustomed to such things here, so I in fact don't know what price it would bring in today. By how much would you have increased your capital when you'd sold your little supply?

F: I still don't understand what you're talking about.

sz: I see in your passport here that you often travel to Turkey. You've been there seven times this year alone.

F: Winkler's arrange tours to Turkey. As a group guide I have to travel there quite often.

sz: Yes, and it suits you very well, doesn't it? In Turkey

hashish is fairly cheap and quite easy to get hold of. Isn't it, Mr. Fröbe?

F: . . . . .

SZ: If you prefer to say nothing it will be the worse for you. We already have enough evidence, and in addition to that a witness.

F: The dirty skunk squealed after all!

SZ: Exactly.

F: That god-damned bastard Swede!

SZ: Perhaps you realize that it is serving no useful purpose to keep this up any longer. Start talking now, Fröbe! I want to hear the whole thing, with all the facts you can remember, names, dates and figures. You can begin by telling me when you began smuggling narcotics.

Fröbe closed his eyes and fell to one side off the chair. Martin Beck saw him put his hand out before he actually fell prostrate onto the floor.

Szluka rose and nodded to the stenographer, who closed the notebook and vanished out the door.

Szluka looked down at the man lying on the floor.

"He's bluffing," said Martin Beck. "He didn't faint."

"I know," said Szluka. "But I'll let him rest for a while before I go on."

He went up to Fröbe and poked him with the tip of his shoe. "Get up, Fröbe."

Fröbe did not move, but his eyelids quivered. Szluka went over to the door, opened it and called out something into the corridor. A policeman came in and Szluka said something to him. The policeman took Fröbe by the arm and Szluka said, "Don't lie there cluttering up the place, Fröbe. We'll get a bunk for you to lie on. It's much more comfortable."

Fröbe got up and looked offendedly at Szluka. Then he limped out behind the policeman. Martin Beck watched him go.

"How is his leg?"

"No danger," said Szluka. "Only a flesh wound. We don't often need to shoot, but when it's necessary, we shoot accurately."

"So that's what he was up to. Hashish smuggling," said Martin Beck. "I wonder what they've done with him."

"Alf Matsson? I expect we'll get it out of them. But it's best to wait until they've had a bit of rest. You must be tired yourself," said Szluka, sitting down behind his desk.

Martin Beck felt very tired indeed. It was already morning. He felt bruised and battered.

"Go back to the hotel and sleep for a few hours," said Szluka. "I'll phone you later. Go down to the entrance and I'll get a car sent around for you."

Martin Beck had no objections. He shook hands with Szluka and left him. As he closed the door behind him, he heard Szluka speaking into the telephone.

The car was already waiting for him when he got down to the street.

19

The cleaning woman had been into his room and switched off the light and closed the shutters. He did not bother to open them again. Now he knew that there would be no tall, dark man outside looking up at his window.

Martin Beck switched on the overhead light and undressed. His head and left arm ached. He looked in the long mirror in the wardrobe. He had a large bruise above his right knee, and his left shoulder was swollen and black and blue. He ran his hand over his head and felt a large bump at the back of it. He could not find any more injuries.

The bed looked soft and cool and inviting. He switched off the light and crept down between the sheets. He lay on his back for a while and tried to think as he stared out into the half-light. Then he turned over on his side and fell asleep.

It was nearly two o'clock when he woke to the sound of the telephone ringing. It was Szluka.

"Have you slept?"

"Yes."

"Good. Can you come over?"

"Yes. Now?"

"I'll send a car. It'll be there in half an hour. Is that all right?"

"Yes. I'll be down in half an hour."

He showered and dressed and opened the shutters. The sun was blazing and the sharp light stung his eyes. He looked toward the quay on the other side of the river. The past night seemed unreal and remote to him.

The car, with the same driver as before, was waiting. He found his way to Szluka's room by himself and knocked before opening the door and going in.

Szluka was alone. He was sitting behind his desk with a sheaf of papers and the indispensable coffee cup in front of him. He nodded and motioned toward the chair Fröbe had sat in. Then he lifted the receiver, said something and put it back again.

"How are you feeling?" he said, looking at Martin Beck.

"Fine. I've slept. And you? How's it going?"

A policeman came in and placed two cups of coffee on the table. Then he took Szluka's empty cup and left.

"It's all finished now. I've got everything here," said Szluka, picking up the sheaf of papers.

"And Alf Matsson?" said Martin Beck.

"Well," said Szluka. "That's the only point that's not clear yet. I haven't managed to get anything there. They insist that they don't know where he is."

"But he was one of the gang?"

"Yes, in a way. He was their middleman. The whole thing was organised by Fröbe and Radeberger. The girl was just used as a sort of clearinghouse for the whole business. Boeck, whatever her first name is."

Szluka fumbled in his papers.

"Ari," said Martin Beck. "Aranka."

"Yes, Ari Boeck. Fröbe and Radeberger had already been smuggling hashish from Turkey some time before they met her. Both of them seem to have had relations with her. After a while, they realized they could use her in another way and told her about the narcotics smuggling. She had no objections to joining in on it. Then they both lived with her when she moved to Újpest. She seems to be a fairly loose sort of creature."

"Yes," said Martin Beck. "I suppose so."

"Radeberger and Fröbe went to Turkey as travel guides. In Turkey they got hold of the hashish, which is quite cheap and easily obtainable there, and then smuggled it into Hungary. It was fairly easy, especially since they were group guides and had to deal with all the luggage belonging to the party. Ari Boeck made contact with the middlemen and helped sell the drugs here in Budapest. Radeberger and Fröbe also traveled to other countries such as Poland, Czechoslovakia, Rumania and Bulgaria with hashish for their pushers."

"And Alf Matsson was one of them?" said Martin Beck.

"Alf Matsson was one of the pushers," said Szluka. "They had some others who came from England, Germany and Holland, either here or to some other East European country where they met Radeberger and Fröbe. They paid in Western currencies—pounds, dollars or marks—and got their hashish, which they then took back home with them and sold there."

"So everyone profited a good deal from the business, except the people who in the end bought the junk to use," said Martin Beck. "It's odd that they've managed to get away with this for so long without being discovered."

Szluka rose and went across to the window. He stood there for a while, his hands behind his back, looking out onto the street. Then he went back and sat down again.

"No," he said. "It's not really that strange. So long as none of the stuff was sold here or in any other socialist country, except to the middlemen, then they had every chance of getting away with it. In the capitalist countries concerned, they don't think there's anything worth smuggling out of Eastern Bloc countries, so customs control hardly exists for travelers from these countries. On the other hand, if they'd tried to find a market for their goods here, they'd have soon been caught. But that wouldn't have been worth their while, either. It's Western currencies they want."

"They must have made a good deal of money," said Martin Beck.

"Yes," said Szluka. "But the pushers made a lot out of it too. The whole thing was quite cleverly organized, actually. If you hadn't come out here looking for Alf Matsson, it might have been a long time before we'd found all this out."

"What do they say about Alf Matsson?"

"They've admitted he was their pusher in Sweden. Over a period of a year he'd bought quite a lot of hashish from them. But they maintain they haven't seen him since May, when he was here to pick up a consignment. He didn't get as much as he wanted at that time, so he'd communicated with Ari Boeck again fairly soon. They say that they'd agreed to meet him here in Budapest almost three weeks ago, but he never turned up. They claim that the stuff hidden in the car was put aside for him."

Martin Beck sat in silence for a moment. Then he said:

"He might have quarreled with them for one reason or another and threatened to report them. Then they might have got scared and done away with him. The way they tried to get rid of me last night."

Szluka sat in silence. After a while Martin Beck went on, quietly, as if talking to himself, "That's what must have happened."

Szluka got up and paced the floor for a bit. Then he said, "That's what I thought had happened too."

He fell silent again and stopped in front of the map.

"What do you think now?" said Martin Beck.

Szluka turned and looked at him.

"I don't know," he said. "I thought perhaps you'd like to talk to one of them yourself. This Radeberger. The one you fought with last night. He's talkative and I have an impression that he's too stupid to be able to lie well. Would you like to question him? Perhaps you'd do better than I did."

"Yes, please," said Martin Beck. "I'd very much like to question him."

20

Tetz Radeberger came into the room. He was dressed as he had been the previous night, in a snug pullover, thin Dacron trousers with elastic at the waist and light, rubber-soled cloth shoes. Dressed to kill. He stopped inside the door and bowed. The policeman escorting him prodded him lightly in the back.

Martin Beck gestured toward the chair on the other side of the desk, and the German sat down. There was an expectant and uncertain look in his deep-blue eyes. He had a bandage on his forehead and there was a blue swelling at his hairline. Otherwise he looked well and strong and fairly intact.

"We're going to talk about Alf Matsson," said Martin Beck.

"I don't know where he is," said Radeberger immediately.

"Possibly. But we're going to talk about him all the same."

Szluka had got out a tape recorder. It was standing on the right of the desk and Martin Beck stretched out his hand and switched it on. The German kept a close watch on his movements.

"When did you meet Alf Matsson for the first time?"

"Two years ago."

"Where?"

"Here in Budapest. At a place called the Ifjuság. A sort of young people's hotel."

"How did you meet him?"

"Through Ari Boeck. She worked there. That was long before she moved to Újpest."

"What happened then?"

"Nothing special. Theo and I had just come back from Turkey. We arranged trips there for tourists. From resorts in Rumania and Bulgaria. We brought a little stuff back with us from Istanbul."

"Had you already begun to smuggle drugs then?"

"Only a little. For our own use, so to speak. But we didn't use it all that often. We never use it now." He paused briefly, and then said, "It's not good for you."

"What did you want it for then?"

"Well, for broads and all that. It's good for broads. They get . . . more . . . inclined . . ."

"Matsson, then? Where does he come into the picture?"

"We offered him some to smoke. He wasn't all that interested either. Drank liquor mostly."

He thought for a moment, and then said foolishly, "That's not good for your body either."

"Did you sell narcotics to Matsson that time?"

"No, but he got a little. We hadn't got all that much. He grew interested when he heard how easy it was to buy in Istanbul."

"Had you yourselves already thought about smuggling on a large scale at that time?"

"We'd talked about it. The difficulty was getting the stuff into the countries where it paid you to sell it."

"Where, for instance?"

"Scandinavia, Holland, at home in Germany. The customs and the police are on the alert there, especially when they know you come from countries like Turkey. Or North Africa and Spain too, for that matter."

"Did Matsson offer to become a pusher?"

"Yes. He said that when you traveled from Eastern Europe, the customs people were hardly ever interested in your luggage, especially if you were flying. It wasn't difficult for us to get the stuff out of Turkey, to here, for instance. We were travel guides, after all. But then we couldn't get much farther with it. The risks were too great. And you can't sell it here. You'd get caught, and anyhow, it isn't worth it."

He thought about this for a moment.

"We didn't want to get caught," he said.

"I can see that. Did you make an agreement with Matsson then?"

"Yes. He had a good idea. We were to meet at different places—ones that suited Theo and me. We let him know and then he went there for his magazine. It was a good cover-up. Looked innocent."

"How did he pay you?"

"In dollars—cash. It was a fine plan, and we built up our organization that summer. Got hold of more pushers—a Dutchman we met in Prague and—"

This was Szluka's department. Martin Beck said, "Where did you and Matsson meet next time?"

"In Constanta, in Rumania, three weeks later. Everything went very smoothly."

"Was Miss Boeck in on it then too?"

"Ari? No, what use would she have been?"

"But she knew what you were doing?"

"Yes, part of it anyhow."

"How many times did you and Matsson meet altogether?"

"Ten, maybe fifteen. It worked beautifully. He always paid what we asked and must have earned a lot himself."

"How much, do you think?"

"Don't know, but he always had plenty of money."

"Where is he now?"

"I don't know."

"Really?"

"Yes, it's true. We met here in May, when Ari had moved to Újpest. He stayed at that young people's hotel. He got a shipment at that point. He said he had a big market, and we decided that we should meet here again on the twenty-third of July."

"And?"

"We came here on the twenty-first. That was a Thursday. But he never turned up."

"He was here in Budapest. He came on the twenty-second in the evening. He left his hotel on the twenty-third, in the morning. Where were you going to meet?"

"In Újpest. At Ari's place."

"So he went there on the twenty-third in the morning."

"No, I tell you. He never turned up. We waited, but he didn't come. Then we phoned the hotel, but he wasn't there."

"Who called?"

"Theo and I did, and Ari. We took turns."

"Did you call from Újpest?"

"No. From different places. He didn't come, I tell you. We sat there waiting."

"You claim you haven't seen him since he came here, in other words?"

"Yes."

"Let's pretend that I believe you. You haven't met Matsson. But that doesn't stop Fröbe or Miss Boeck from having contacted him, does it?"

"No, I know they haven't."

"How do you know that?"

Radeberger's expression began to grow slightly desperate. He was sweating freely. It was very hot in the room.

"Now listen," he said. "I don't know what you think, but that other man seems to believe we got rid of him. But why should we do that? We made money off him, a lot of money."

"Did you give Miss Boeck money too?"

"Oh, yes. She helped and got her share. Enough so that she didn't have to work."

Martin Beck stared at the man for a long time. Finally he said, "Did you kill him?"

"No, I keep telling you. Would we have stayed on here for

three weeks with nearly that whole supply of stuff if we'd done that?"

His voice had grown shrill and tense.

"Did you like Alf Matsson?"

The man's eyes flickered.

"Please answer when I ask you something," said Martin Beck seriously.

"Of course."

"Miss Boeck appears to have said at her interrogation that neither you nor Theo Fröbe liked Matsson."

"He was nasty when he drank. He . . . despised us because we were Germans."

He turned an appealing blue look upon Martin Beck and said, "And that's not fair, is it?"

There was a silent pause. Tetz Radeberger did not like it. He fidgeted and pulled nervously at the joints of his fingers.

"We haven't killed anyone," he said. "We're not that kind."

"You tried to kill me last night."

"That was different."

The man said this in such a low voice that his words were almost inaudible.

"In what way?"

"It was our only chance."

"Chance to what? To be hanged? Or to get a life sentence in prison?"

The German gave him a shattered look.

"You'll probably get that anyway," said Martin Beck, in a friendly way. "Have you been to prison before?"

"Yes. At home."

"Well, what did you mean by your only chance being to try to kill me?"

"Don't you see? When you came to Újpest and had his— Matsson's—passport with you, we thought at first that he hadn't been able to come and had sent you instead. But you didn't say anything, and besides you weren't the right type. So Matsson must have been caught and spilled the beans. But we didn't know who you were. We'd already been here twenty days, and we had the whole consignment lying around, and we were getting nervous about it. And after three weeks we'd have to get our visas extended. So Theo followed you when you went and . . ."

"Yes, go on."

"And I took the car apart and hid the stuff. Theo couldn't figure out who you were, so we agreed that Ari should find out. The next day, Theo followed you to those baths. He phoned Ari from there and she went and watched for you outside. Then Theo saw you together with that guy in the pool. Afterward he followed the other guy and saw him go into the police station. So it was obvious. All that afternoon and evening we waited and nothing happened. We figured you hadn't said anything yet or else the police would already have been there. Then Ari came back during the night."

"What had she found out?"

"I don't know, but it was something. She just said, 'Fix that bastard, and quick.' She was in a bad mood. Then she went into her room and slammed the door behind her."

"Oh?"

"Next day we watched you all the time. We were in a hell of a situation. We had to keep you quiet before you went to the police. We didn't get a chance and had almost given up hope when you went out in the night. Theo followed you across the bridge and I drove around with the car across the other bridge, Lanc-híd. Then we changed over. Theo didn't dare do it. And I'm the strongest. I've always looked after my body."

He fell silent for a moment then said appealingly, as if this were some excuse, "We didn't know you were the police."

Martin Beck did not reply.

"Are you a policeman?"

"Yes, I'm a policeman. Let's go back to Alf Matsson. You said that you met him through Miss Boeck. Had they known each other long?"

"Awhile. Ari had been on some athletic team in Sweden, swimming, and she met him there. Then she wasn't allowed to swim any more, but he looked her up when he came here."

"Are Matsson and Miss Boeck good friends?"

"Fairly."

"Do they often have intimate relations with each other?"

"Do you mean do they sleep together? Of course."

"Do you sleep with Miss Boeck too?"

"Of course. When I feel like it. Theo too. Ari is a nymphomaniac. There's not much you can do about it. Obviously Matsson slept with her when he was here. Once we all three had a go at her, in the same room. Ari does anything in that line. Otherwise she's a good girl."

"Good?"

"Yes, she does what you tell her. As long as you fuck her now and then. I don't do it so much now. It's not really very good for you to do it too much. But Theo is always at it. So he's got no energy for anything."

"Have you never quarreled with Matsson?"

"About Ari? She's nothing to fight over."

"But about other things?"

"Not about business. He was good at the business."

"Otherwise then?"

"Once he kicked up such a fuss I had to smack him. He was drunk at the time, of course. Then Ari took him in hand and calmed him down. That was a long time ago."

"Where do you think Matsson is now?"

Radeberger shook his head helplessly.

"I don't know. Here somewhere."

"Didn't he associate with other people here?"

"He just came, collected his consignment and paid. And then he did some kind of magazine article to make it all watertight. Three or four days later he went back."

Martin Beck sat silently for a while, looking at the man who had tried to kill him.

"I think that'll do now," he said, switching off the tape recorder.

Evidently the German still had something on his mind.

"Say, that business yesterday . . . Can you forgive me?"

"No. I can't. Good-bye."

He made a sign to the policeman, who rose, took Radeberger by the arm and led him toward the door. Martin Beck watched the blond Teuton thoughtfully. Then he said, "One moment, Herr Radeberger. This is nothing to do with me personally. Yesterday you tried to murder a person to save your own skin. You had planned the murder as best you could and it was no thanks to you that it didn't succeed. That's not only illegal, but it's also a breach of a basic rule of life and an important principle. That's why it's unforgivable. That's all. Think about it."

Martin Beck rewound the tape, put it into the cassette and returned to Szluka.

"I think you're probably right. Perhaps they haven't killed him."

"No," said Szluka. "It doesn't seem like it. We've got all the stops out now, looking for him."

"So have we."

"Has your assignment become official yet?"

"Not so far as I know."

Szluka scratched the back of his neck.

"Peculiar," he said.

"What?"

"That we can't locate him."

Half an hour later, Martin Beck returned to his hotel. It was already time for dinner. Dusk fell over the Danube, and on the other side of the river he saw the quay and the stone wall and the steps.

21

Martin Beck had just finished dressing and was on his way to the dining room when the telephone rang.

"From Stockholm," said the telephone operator. "A Mr. Eriksson."

The name was familiar to him: it was Alf Matsson's boss, the editor in chief of the aggressive weekly.

A pompous voice came over the line.

"That's Beck, is it? This is Eriksson, the editor in chief here."

"This is Inspector Beck."

The man ignored this and went on. "Well, as you are probably aware, I know all about your assignment. I was the one to put you on the track. And I've good connections with the Foreign Office, too."

So his hideous namesake had not been able to keep his mouth shut either.

"Are you still there?"

"Yes."

"Perhaps we'd better be a little careful what we say, if you know what I mean. But first I must ask: have you found the man you're looking for?"

"Matsson? No, not yet."

"No clue at all?"

"No."

"It's absolutely unheard-of."

"Yes."

"Well, how can I put it now . . . How's the atmosphere down there?"

"It's hot. A little misty in the mornings."

"What d'you say? Misty in the mornings? Yes, I think I understand. Yes, exactly. Now, however, I think the time has come when in all good conscience we can't keep this thing under wraps any longer. Why, what's happened is perfectly incredible—it could lead to dreadful things. We have a great responsibility for Matsson personally too. He's one of our best people, an excellent man, thoroughly honest and loyal. I've had him on my general staff for a couple of years now, and I know what I'm talking about."

"Where?"

"What?"

"Where have you had him?"

"Oh, that. On my general staff. We say that, you know. Editorial general staff. I know what I'm talking about. I'd stake my life on that man and that makes my responsibility even greater."

Martin Beck stood thinking about something else. He was trying to imagine what Eriksson looked like. Probably a fat, bumptious little man with pig eyes and a red beard.

"So today I've decided to publish our first article on the Alf Matsson case in next week's issue. This coming Monday, without further delay. The moment has come to focus public attention on this story. I just wanted to know whether you'd found any trace of him, as I said."

"I think you should take your article and—"

Martin Beck stopped himself just in time and said, ". . . throw it into the wastebasket."

"What? What did you say? I don't understand."

"Read the papers in the morning," said Martin Beck and put down the receiver.

His appetite had vanished during the conversation. He took out his bottle and poured himself a stiff whisky. Then he sat down and thought. He was in a bad temper and had a headache, and on top of that he had been discourteous. But that was not what he was thinking about.

Alf Matsson had come to Budapest on the twenty-second of July. He had been seen at the passport control. He had taken a taxi to the Hotel Ifjuság and stayed there for one night. Someone at the reception desk must have dealt with him. The following morning, Saturday the twenty-third, he had, again by taxi, moved to the Hotel Duna and stayed there for half an hour. At about ten o'clock in the morning he had gone out. The people at the reception desk had noticed him.

After that, as far as was known, no one had seen or spoken to Alf Matsson. He had left one single clue behind him: the key to his hotel room, which, according to Szluka, had been found on the steps outside the police station.

Assuming that Fröbe and Radeberger were telling the truth, he had not turned up at the meeting place in Újpest and, consequently, they had not been able either to kidnap or kill him.

So for some unknown reason, Alf Matsson had gone up in smoke.

The existing material was extremely thin but, nevertheless, it was all there was to work on.

Five people, it was established, had had contact with Alf Matsson on Hungarian soil and could be regarded as witnesses.

A passport officer, two taxi drivers and two hotel receptionists.

If something wholly unexpected had happened to him—if, for instance, he had been attacked, kidnapped or killed in an accident or gone insane—then their testimonies were useless. But, on the other hand, if he had made himself invisible of his own free will, then those people might have observed some detail in his appearance or behavior which might be important to the investigation.

Martin Beck had personally been in contact with two of these hypothetical witnesses. Considering the language difficulties, however, it was uncertain whether he had been able to exploit them fully. Neither the taxi drivers nor the passport official could be located, and even if he found them, he would presumably not be able to speak to them.

The only substantial material he had to go on was Matsson's passport and luggage. Neither told him anything.

This was his summary of the Alf Matsson case. Extremely depressing insofar as it showed that, as far as he was concerned, the investigation had ended in complete deadlock. If, despite everything, Matsson's disappearance was connected with the gang of smugglers—and it was difficult to believe that it was *not*—then Szluka would sooner or later clear the matter up. In that case, the best support he could give the Hungarian police would be to go home, bring in the Narcotics Squad and help wind up the Swedish end of the case.

Martin Beck came to a decision and converted it immediately into action by means of two telephone calls.

First, the well-dressed young man from the Swedish Embassy.

"Have you managed to find him?"

"No."

"Nothing new, in other words."

"Matsson was a narcotics smuggler. The Hungarian police are looking for him. For our part, we'll put out a description through Interpol."

"How very unpleasant."

"Yes."

"And what is this going to mean for you?"

"That I go home. Tomorrow, if it can be arranged. I'd like some help with that little matter."

"It may be difficult, but I'll do my best."

"Yes, do that. It's very important."

"I'll phone early tomorrow morning."

"Thank you."

"Good-bye. I hope you've had a nice time these few days, all the same."

"Yes, very nice. Good-bye."

After that, Szluka. He was at police headquarters.

"I'm going back to Sweden tomorrow."

"Oh, yes. Have a good trip."

"You'll get our report eventually."

"And you'll get ours. We've still not found Matsson."

"Are you surprised?"

"Very. Frankly, I've never seen anything like it. But we'll get him soon."

"Have you checked the camping sites?"

"We're doing that. Takes a little time. Fröbe's tried to kill himself, by the way."

"And?"

"Didn't succeed, of course. He threw himself at the wall head first. Got a bump on his skull. I've had him transferred to the psychiatric department. The doctor says he's a manic-depressive. The question is whether we'll have to let the girl go the same way."

"And Radeberger?"

"All right. Asking whether there's a gymnasium in the prison. There is."

"Could I ask you something?"

"Go ahead."

"We know that Matsson had contact with five people here in Budapest from Friday evening until Saturday morning."

"Two hotel receptionists and two taxi drivers. Where do we get the fifth from?"

"The passport control officer."

"My only excuse is that I haven't been home for thirty-six hours. So you want him questioned?"

"Yes. Everything he can remember. What he said, how he behaved, what he was wearing."

"I see."

"Can you get the report done in German or English and air-mail it to Stockholm?"

"Telex is better. Anyhow, perhaps there'll be time to get it to you before you leave."

"Hardly. I'll probably be going about eleven."

"We're famous for our speed. The wife of the Minister of Trade had her bag snatched at Nep Stadium last autumn. She took a taxi here to report it. When she got here, she was handed back her bag at the desk downstairs. That kept us in good shape for a long time. Well, we'll see."

"Thanks then. And good-bye."

"Good-bye. Pity there wasn't time to meet a little more informally."

Martin Beck paused briefly to think. Then he set up a call to Stockholm. The call came through in ten minutes.

"Lennart's away," said Kollberg's wife. "As usual, he didn't say where he was going. 'Duty calls, be back on Sunday, take care of yourself.' He took the car with him. To hell with police-men."

Melander next. This time it took only five minutes.

"Hi! Did I disturb you?"

"I'd just gone to bed."

Melander was famous for his memory, his ten hours' sleep a night and a singular capacity for constantly being in the W. C.

"Are you in on the Matsson case?"

"Yeah."

"Find out what he did the night before he left. In detail. How he behaved, what he said, what he was wearing."

"Tonight?"

"Tomorrow will do."

"Uh-huh."

"Bye, then."

"Bye."

Martin Beck had finished with the telephone. He took pen and paper and went downstairs.

Alf Matsson's luggage was still standing in the room behind the reception desk.

He took the cover off the typewriter, placed it on the table, inserted a piece of paper in the machine and typed:

> Portable typewriter, Erika, with case
> Yellowish-brown pigskin suitcase with strap, fairly new

He opened the case and set its contents out on the table. He then went on typing.

> Gray-and-black checked shirt
> Sport shirt, brown
> White poplin shirt, fresh-laundered, Metro Laundry, Stockholm
> Light-gray gabardine trousers, well-pressed
> Three handkerchiefs, white
> Four pairs socks, brown, dark-blue, light-gray, wine-red
> Two pairs colored undershorts, green-and-white check
> One fishnet undershirt
> One pair light-brown suede shoes

He looked gloomily at the cardigan-like garment, picked it up and went out to the girl at the reception desk. She was very pretty, in a sweet, ordinary way. Rather small, well built, long fingers, pretty calves, fine ankles, a few dark hairs on her shins, long thighs under her skirt. No rings. He stared at her with his thoughts far away.

"What's this kind of thing called?" he said.

"A jersey blazer," she said.

He remained standing there, thinking about something. The girl blushed. She moved to the other end of the reception desk, adjusting her skirt and pulling at her bra and girdle. He could not understand why. He went back, sat down at the table and typed:

> Dark blue jersey blazer
> 58 sheets typing paper, legal size
> One typewriter eraser
> Electric shaver, Remington
> *The Night Wanderer* by Kurt Salomonson
> Shaving kit
> Shaving lotion, Tabac
> Tube of toothpaste, Squibb, opened
> Toothbrush
> Mouthwash, Vademecum
> Aspirin with codeine, box unopened
> Dark-blue plastic wallet
> $1500 in $20 bills
> Skr 600 in hundred-kronor notes, new type
> Typed on Alf Matsson's typewriter

He repacked all the things, folded the list and left. The girl at the reception desk looked at him in confusion. Now she appeared prettier than ever.

Martin Beck went into the dining room and ate a late dinner, with an absent-minded expression still on his face.

The waiter put a Swedish flag in front of him. The maestro came up to his table and played a patriotic Swedish melody in his left ear. He did not seem to notice it.

He drank his coffee in one gulp, put a red hundred-forint note on the table without even waiting for the bill and went upstairs to bed.

22

It was just a few minutes past nine o'clock when the young man from the Embassy telephoned.

"You're in luck," he said. "I've managed to get a seat on the plane that leaves Budapest at twelve o'clock. You get to Prague at ten to two and you have five minutes to wait before the SAS plane to Copenhagen leaves."

"Thanks," said Martin Beck.

"It wasn't easy to arrange at such short notice. Can you pick up the tickets yourself at Malev's? I've arranged for the payment of them, so they can just be collected."

"Naturally," said Martin Beck. "Thanks very much indeed."

"Have a nice flight then, Mr. Beck. It's been very pleasant having you here."

"Thank you," said Martin Beck. "Good-bye."

As predicted the tickets were waiting for him, with the dark curly-haired beauty he had spoken to three days earlier.

He returned to his hotel room, packed his bag and sat at the window for a while, smoking and looking out over the river. Then he left the room (in which he had stayed for five days and Alf Matsson had stayed for half an hour), went down to reception and ordered a taxi. As he came outside onto the steps, he saw a blue-and-white police car approaching at great speed. It braked in front of the hotel, and a uniformed policeman whom he had not seen before leaped out and hurried through the revolving doors. Martin had time to see that he had an envelope in his hand.

His taxi swung around and stopped behind the police car, and the doorman with the gray mustache opened the back door. Martin Beck asked him to wait and went back into the revolving doors just as the policeman went into them from the other direction, closely followed by the receptionist. When the receptionist caught sight of Martin Beck, he waved and pointed to the policeman. After having whirled around a couple of times in the revolving doors, they all three succeeded in meeting up on the hotel steps and Martin Beck was given his envelope. He stepped into the taxi after having given out his last aluminum coins to the receptionist and the doorman.

On the plane, he was seated beside a boastful, loud-voiced Englishman, who hung over him, spraying saliva into his face as he related stories about his totally uninteresting activities as some kind of commercial traveler.

In Prague, Martin Beck just had time to rush through the transit hall into the next plane, before it took off. To his relief the expectorating Englishman was nowhere to be seen, and when they were up in the air, he opened the envelope.

Szluka and his men had done their best to live up to their reputation for speed. They had questioned six witnesses and done the report in English. Martin Beck read:

> Summary of interrogation of those persons known by the police to have had contact with the Swedish citizen Alf Sixten Matsson from the time of his arrival at Ferihegyi Airport in Budapest at 10:15 P.M. on July 22, 1966, until his disappearance from Hotel Duna in Budapest at unknown time between 10:00 A.M. and 11:00 A.M. on July 23 of the same year.
>
> *Ferenc Havas*, passport control officer who was on duty alone at the passport control point at Ferihegyi on the night between July 22 and July 23, 1966, says that he does not remember seeing Alf Matsson.
>
> *János Lucacs*, taxi driver, says that he remembers that on the night between July 22 and 23 he took a passenger from Ferihegyi to Hotel Ifjuság. According to Lucacs, the passenger was a man between 25 and 30 years of age, had a beard and spoke German. Lucacs, who does not speak German, under-

stood only that the man wanted to be taken to Ifjuság. Lucacs thinks he remembers that the man had a suitcase, which he put down beside him on the back seat.

Léo Szabo, medical student, night porter at Hotel Ifjuság on July 22–23, remembers a man who came to the hotel late one evening between July 17–24. Everything indicates that this man was Alf Matsson although Szabo remembers neither the exact time of the man's arrival, nor his name or nationality. According to Szabo, the man was between 30 and 35 years old, spoke good English and had a beard. He was wearing light-colored trousers, blue jacket, probably a white shirt, and tie, and had light luggage—one or two bags. Szabo cannot remember having seen this man on any other occasion but this one.

Béla Péter, taxi driver, drove Alf Matsson from the Hotel Ifjuság to the Hotel Duna on the morning of July 23. He remembers a young man with a brown beard and glasses, whose luggage consisted of one large and one smaller bag, the smaller probably a typewriter.

Béla Kovacs, porter at the Hotel Duna, received Matsson's passport and gave him the key to Room 105 on the morning of July 23. According to Kovacs, Matsson was then wearing light, probably gray trousers, white shirt, blue jacket and a plain-colored tie. He was carrying a light-colored coat over his arm.

Eva Petrovich, receptionist at the same hotel, saw Matsson both when he arrived at the hotel shortly before 10:00 A.M. on July 23, and when he left the hotel about half an hour later. She has given the most extensive description of Matsson and maintains she is certain about all details, except the color of his tie. According to Miss Petrovich, Matsson was of medium height, had blue eyes, dark-brown hair, beard and mustache and steel-rimmed glasses. He was wearing light-gray trousers, dark-blue summer blazer, white shirt, blue or red tie, and beige shoes. Over his arm he had a light-beige poplin coat.

Szluka had added something:

As you see we have not found out much more than what we already knew. None of the witnesses can remember anything special that Matsson did or said. I have added the description of his clothing at his disappearance to the personal description

we have sent all over the country. Should any other facts come to light, I shall let you know immediately. Have a good trip!
Vilmos Szluka

Martin Beck read through Szluka's summary again. He wondered whether Eva Petrovich was the same girl who had helped him identify the cardigan-like garment in Alf Matsson's suitcase. On the back of Szluka's letter, he wrote:

> Light-gray trousers
> White shirt
> Dark-blue blazer
> Red or blue tie
> Beige shoes
> Light-beige poplin coat

Then he took out the list he had made of the contents of Alf Matsson's bag and read through it before putting everything into his briefcase and closing it.

He leaned back in his seat and closed his eyes. He did not sleep, but sat like this until the plane began to go down through the thin cloud bank over Copenhagen.

Kastrup was as usual. He had to stand in a line before being sluiced into the transit hall, where people of all nationalities were crowding in front of the counters. He drank a Tuborg in the bar to gather his strength before tackling the trying task of collecting his luggage.

It was past three o'clock when he finally stood with his bag outside the airport building. A whole row of taxis was standing in the stand and he put his bag in the first one, got into the front seat and gave the driver the address of the harbor in Dragør.

The ferry, which was in and appeared ready to leave, was called *Drogden* and was an unusually ugly creation. Martin Beck put his bag and briefcase down in the cafeteria and went up on deck as the ferry eased its way out and headed for Sweden.

After the heat of the last few days in Budapest, the breeze in the Sound felt cold and after a while Martin Beck went in and sat down in the cafeteria. There were a great many people on board, mostly housewives who had been shopping over in Denmark.

The trip took scarcely an hour, and in Limhamn he at once got a taxi that would take him to Malmö. The taxi driver was talkative and spoke a southern Swedish dialect that sounded to Martin Beck almost as incomprehensible as Hungarian.

23

The taxi stopped outside the police station on David-hall Square. Martin Beck got out, walked up the wide steps and deposited his bag in the glass reception office. He had not been there for two years but was struck, as always, by the massiveness and majestic solemnity of the building and by its pompous halls and wide corridors. Two flights up, he stopped in front of a door marked INSPECTOR, knocked and slipped in. Someone had once said that Martin Beck knew the art of standing inside a room having already shut the door behind him at the same time as he knocked on it from the outside. There was a grain of truth in this.

"Hiya," he said.

There were two people in the room. One of them was standing leaning against the window, chewing a toothpick. He was very large. The other, who was sitting at the desk, was tall and thin, with his hair brushed straight back and his eyes lively. Both were in civilian clothes. The man at the desk looked critically at Martin Beck and said, "Quarter of an hour ago I read in the paper that you were abroad, breaking up international narcotics rings. And now you just walk in here saying hiya. Is that any way to behave? Do you want something?"

"Do you remember a stabbing case here on the eve of Twelfth Day? Guy called Matsson?"

"No. Should I?"

"I remember it," said the man by the window, apathetically.

"This is Månsson," said the Inspector. "He does . . . what are you doing, actually, Månsson?"

"Nothing. I was just thinking of going home."

"Exactly. He isn't doing anything and was thinking of going home. Well, what is it you remember?"

"I've forgotten."

"Is there any other way you can be of service?"

"Not until Monday. I'm off duty now."

"Must you munch like that?"

"I'm giving up smoking."

"What do you remember about that stabbing case?"

"Nothing."

"Nothing at all?"

"No. Backlund was in charge."

"What did he think, then?"

"Don't know. He worked hard on the preliminary investigation for several days. Was very secretive about it."

"You're very lucky," said the man at the desk to Martin Beck.

"Why?"

"Well, to be allowed to meet Backlund," said Månsson.

"Exactly. He's popular. Coming back in half an hour. Room 312. Take a ticket for the queue."

"Thanks."

"This Matsson, is he the same guy you're looking for?"

"Yes."

"Was he here in Malmö?"

"I don't think so."

"They're no fun," said Månsson mournfully.

"What aren't?"

"Toothpicks."

"Then for God's sake, smoke. No one asked you to eat toothpicks."

"They say there's a kind with taste to them," said Månsson.

Martin Beck recognized the lingo only too well. Something had probably wrecked their day. Their wives had no doubt called and pointed out that their food was spoiling and inquired whether there were no other policemen.

He left them to their troubles, went up to the canteen and had a cup of tea. He took out Szluka's paper from his inside pocket and read through the meager testimonies once again. Somewhere behind him there was an exchange of remarks.

"Excuse me for asking, but is this really a mazarine cupcake?"

"What else do you think it is?"

"Some kind of cultural monument, maybe. Seems a pity to eat it. The Bakery Museum ought to be interested."

"If you don't like it, you can go somewhere else."

"Yeah, two floors down for instance, and report you for harboring dangerous weapons. I order a mazarine cupcake and you go and give me a fossilized fetus that not even the Swedish State Railway would serve up without the locomotive blushing. I'm a sensitive person and—"

"Sensitive, eh? And by the way, you took it off the counter yourself."

Martin Beck turned around and looked at Kollberg.

"Hi," he said.

"Hi."

Neither of them seemed particularly surprised. Kollberg pushed away the objectionable cake and said, "When did you get back?"

"This moment. What are you doing here?"

"I thought I'd talk to someone named Backlund."

"Me too."

"Actually, I had something else to do here," said Kollberg apologetically.

Ten minutes later it was five o'clock. They went down together. Backlund turned out to be an elderly man with a friendly, ordinary face. He shook hands and said:

"Oh, yes. VIP's from Stockholm, eh?"

He put out two chairs for them and sat down, saying:

"Well, I am grateful. To what do I owe this honor?"

"You had a stabbing case on the eve of Twelfth Day," said Kollberg. "A guy called Matsson."

"Yes, that's quite correct. I remember the case. It's closed. No charge brought."

"What really happened?" said Martin Beck.

"Well, hm-m . . . Wait a minute and I'll get the file."

The man called Backlund went out and returned about ten minutes later with a typed report stapled together. It seemed remarkably detailed. He leafed through it for a moment, evidently renewing his acquaintance with it with both delight and pride. Finally he said, "We'd better take it from the beginning."

"We only want a general idea of what happened," said Kollberg.

"I see. At 1:23 A.M. on January 6 of this year a radio patrol consisting of Patrolman Kristiansson and Patrolman Kvant—who were patrolling in their car on Linnégatan here in town—received orders to go to Sveagatan 26 in Limhamn, where someone was said to have been stabbed. Patrolmen Kristiansson and Kvant at once went to this address, where they arrived at about 1:29 A.M. They took charge of a person who stated that he was a journalist: one Alf Sixten Matsson, residing in Stockholm at Fleminggatan 34. Matsson also stated that he had been assaulted and stabbed by Bengt Eilert Jönsson, a journalist who is a resident of Malmö and lives at Sveagatan 26 in Limhamn. Matsson, who had a flesh wound approximately two inches long on the outside of his left wrist, was taken to the emergency ward of General Hospital by Patrolmen Kristiansson and Kvant while Bengt Eilert Jönsson was held and taken to police headquarters in Malmö by Patrolmen Elofsson and Borglund, who had been called in by Patrolmen Kristiansson and Kvant. Both men were under the influence of alcohol."

"Kristiansson and Kvant?"

Backlund gave Kollberg a look of reproach and went on:

"After Matsson had been treated at the emergency ward of

General Hospital, he was also taken to testify at police head-quarters in Malmö. Matsson stated that he was born on August 5, 1933, in Mölndal and was a resident of—"

"Just a minute," said Martin Beck. "We don't really need all the details."

"Oh. But I must tell you, it isn't easy to get a clear picture if you don't go through it all."

"Does that report give a clear picture?"

"I can answer both yes and no to that question. The stories differ considerably. Times too. The testimonies are very vague. That's why there was no charge brought."

"Who questioned Matsson?"

"I did. I questioned him very thoroughly."

"Was he drunk?"

Backlund leafed through the report.

"One moment. Yes, here it is. He admitted to consuming alcohol, but denied that he had done so in excess."

"How did he behave?"

"I didn't make a note of that. But Kristiansson said—here, just a second—that his walk was unsteady and his voice was calm but occasionally slurred."

Martin Beck gave up. Kollberg was more obstinate.

"What did he look like?"

"I didn't make any kind of note on that. But I remember that his apparel was neat and tidy."

"What happened when he was stabbed?"

"It can be said that it is difficult to get a clear picture of the actual course of events. Their stories differ. If I remember rightly—yes, that's right—Matsson stated that the injury was inflicted upon him at about midnight. On the other hand, Jönsson stated that the incident did not occur until after one o'clock. It was very difficult to get this point cleared up."

"Had he been assaulted?"

"I have Jönsson's statement here. Bengt Eilert Jönsson states that he and Matsson, whom he met through his profession, had been acquaintances for almost three years, and on the morning of January 5 he happened to meet Matsson, who was staying at the Savoy Hotel and was alone, so Jönsson invited him home to dinner, to commence at—"

"Yes, but what did he say about the assault itself?"

Backlund now began to appear a trifle irritated. He turned over a few more pages.

"Jönsson denies intentional assault, but admits that at one fifteen he gave Matsson a shove, at which the latter may have fallen over and cut himself on a glass which he had been holding in his hand."

"But had he been stabbed?"

"Well, that question is dealt with in an earlier section. I'll have a look. Here it is. Matsson states that some time before eleven P.M. he had a scuffle with Bengt Jönsson and thus, probably from a knife he had previously seen in Jönsson's home, he received an injury to his left arm. You can see for yourselves. Just before eleven P.M.! A quarter past one! A difference of two hours and twenty minutes! We also received a certificate from the doctor at the General Hospital. He describes the injury as a two-inch flesh wound, which was bleeding freely. The edges of the wound—"

Kollberg leaned forward and stared hard at the man with the report.

"We're not so interested in all that. What do you think yourself? Something happened, anyway. Why? And how did it come about?"

The other man could now conceal his irritation no longer. He removed his glasses and cleaned them feverishly.

"Oh now, please—please," he said. " 'Happened.' Hm-mph. Everything is examined thoroughly here in these preliminary investigations. If I can't present an account of it all, then I don't see how I can clearly explain the case for you. You can go through the material for yourselves if you like."

He put the report down on the edge of the desk. Martin Beck leafed through it listlessly and looked at the photographs of the scene of the crime attached at the back. The photos showed a kitchen, a living room and some stone stairs. Everything was clean and tidy. On the stairs there were a few dark spots, hardly bigger than a one-öre piece. If they had not been marked with white arrows, they would have been scarcely visible. He handed the document over to Kollberg, drummed his fingers on the arm of the chair and said, "Was Matsson questioned here?"

"Yes, here in this room."

"You must have talked for a long time."

"Yes, he had to give a detailed statement."

"What sort of impression did he make—as a person, I mean?"

Backlund was now so irritated that he could not sit still. He kept moving the objects on the bare varnished surface of his desk and putting them back in exactly the same places.

"Impression!" he said. "Everything is covered thoroughly in the preliminary investigation. I've already told you that. Anyhow, the incident occurred on private property and when it came down to it, Matsson did not wish to bring a charge. I cannot understand what it is you want to know."

Kollberg put down the report without even having opened it. Then he made one last attempt.

"We want to know your personal opinion of Alf Matsson."

"I haven't got one," said the man.

When they left him, he was sitting at his desk reading the report of the preliminary investigation, his expression stiff and disapproving.

"Some people," said Kollberg in the elevator.

24

Bengt Jönsson's house was a rather small bungalow with an open veranda and a garden. The gate was open and on the gravel path inside was a blond, suntanned man, poised on his haunches in front of a tricycle. His hands were covered with grease and he was trying to repair the chain, which had come off. A boy of about five was standing watching him, a wrench in his hand.

When Kollberg and Martin Beck came through the gate, the man rose and wiped his hands on the back of his trousers. He was about thirty and wearing a checked shirt, dirty khaki trousers and wooden-soled shoes.

"Bengt Jönsson?" said Kollberg.

"Yes, that's me."

The man looked at them suspiciously.

"We're from the Stockholm police," said Martin Beck. "We've come to ask for some information about a friend of yours—Alf Matsson."

"Friend," said the man. "I'd hardly call him that. Is it about what happened last winter? I thought that was all dead and buried a long time ago."

"Yes, it is. The case is closed and won't be taken up again. It's not your part in the affair we're interested in, but Alf Matsson's," said Martin Beck.

"I saw in the papers that he's disappeared," said Bengt Jönsson. "He was in on some kind of narcotics ring, it said. I didn't know he used drugs."

"Perhaps he didn't, either. He sold them."

"Oh, Christ," said Bengt Jönsson. "What sort of information do you want? I don't know anything about that drug business."

"You can help us get a general picture of him," said Martin Beck.

"What do you want to know?" asked the fair-haired man.

"Everything you know about Alf Matsson," said Kollberg.

"That's not much," said Jönsson. "I hardly knew him, although we'd been acquainted for three years. I'd only met him a few times before that time last winter. I'm a journalist too, and we met when we were on a job together."

"Would you tell us what really happened last winter?" said Martin Beck.

"We might as well sit down," said Jönsson, going up onto the veranda. Martin Beck and Kollberg followed him. There were a table and four basket chairs, and Martin Beck sat down and offered Jönsson a cigarette. Kollberg looked at his chair suspiciously before cautiously sitting down in it. The chair creaked precariously beneath his weight.

"You'll understand that what you tell us is of no interest to us except as a testimony on Alf Matsson's character. Neither we nor the Malmö police have any reason to take up the case again," said Martin Beck. "What happened?"

"I met Alf Matsson by chance in the street. He was staying at a hotel in Malmö and I invited him home to dinner. I didn't really like him much, but he was on his own in town and wanted me to go out drinking with him, so I thought it'd be better if he came out to our place. He came in a taxi and I think he was sober then. Almost, anyhow. Then we ate and I offered him schnapps with the food and both of us drank quite a bit. After the meal we listened to records and drank whisky and sat talking. He got drunk pretty quickly and then he was unpleasant. My wife had a friend in at the same time and suddenly Alfie said to her, "Say, d'you mind if I fuck you?"

Bengt Jönsson fell silent, and Martin Beck nodded and said, "Go on."

"Well, that's what he said. My wife's friend was very upset, because she's not at all used to being spoken to like that. And my wife got angry and told Alfie he was a boor, and then he called my wife a whore and was damned rude. Then I got angry and told him to watch his mouth and the girls went into another room."

He fell silent again and Kollberg asked, "Was he usually unpleasant like that when he was drunk?"

"I don't know. I'd never seen him drunk before."

"What happened then?" said Martin Beck.

"Well, then we went on drinking. I didn't drink all that much myself, in fact, and didn't feel high at all. But Alfie got drunker and drunker, sitting there, hiccuping and belching and singing, and then suddenly he vomited all over the floor. I got him out to the bathroom and after a while he was all right again and appeared a bit more sober. When I said we should try to wipe up the mess, he said, 'That whore you're married to can do that.' That made me really mad and I told him he'd have to go, that I didn't want him in the house. But he just laughed and sat belching in the chair. When I said I was going to phone for a taxi for him, he said he was going to stay and sleep with my wife. Then I hit him and when he got up and said something dirty about my wife again, I hit him one more time so that he fell over the table and broke two glasses. Then I went on trying to get him out of the house, but he refused to go. Finally my wife called the police—it seemed the only way to get rid of him."

"He injured his hand, I understand," said Kollberg. "How did that happen?"

"I saw he was bleeding, but I didn't think it was serious. I was so angry, anyway, I didn't care. He cut himself on a glass when he fell. Then he claimed I'd stabbed him, which was a lie. I didn't have a knife. Then I was questioned at the police station for the rest of the night. A hellish business all around."

"Have you met Alf Matsson since that night?" said Kollberg.

"Oh, good God, no. Not since that morning at the police station. He was sitting in the corridor when I came out from seeing that cop—sorry, policeman—who was questioning me. And then that bastard had the nerve to say, "Hey, you've got a bit left. Let's go back to your place and finish it off later." I didn't even answer and thank God, I haven't seen him since."

Bengt Jönsson rose and went down to the boy, who was standing hitting the tricycle with the wrench. He crouched down and went on working on the chain.

"I've nothing else to tell you about it all. That was exactly what happened," he said over his shoulder.

Martin Beck and Kollberg got up, and he nodded to them as they went out through the gate.

On the way into Malmö, Kollberg said, "Nice guy, our friend Matsson. I don't think humanity has suffered any great loss if something really has happened to him. If so, then it's only your holiday that suffered."

25

Kollberg was staying at the St. Jörgen Hotel on
Gustav Adolf's Square, so after they had picked up Martin
Beck's suitcase at the police station, they went there. The hotel
was full, but Kollberg used his powers of persuasion and it was
not long before he had arranged for a room.

Martin Beck did not bother to unpack his suitcase. He considered phoning his wife out on the island, but realized that it
was too late. She would hardly be pleased at having to row
across the sound in the dark in order to hear him tell her that
he did not know when he could get there.

He undressed and went into the bathroom. As he stood under
the shower, he heard Kollberg's characteristic thumping on the
door to the corridor. As he had forgotten to take the key out
from the outside, a second or two elapsed before Kollberg
rushed into the room, calling out to him.

Martin Beck turned off the shower, swept a bath towel
around himself and went out to Kollberg.

"A dreadful thought suddenly occurred to me," said Kollberg. "It's five days since the opening of the crayfish season and
you probably haven't had a single one. Or do they have crayfish
in Hungary?"

"Not so far as I know," said Martin Beck. "I didn't see any."

"Get yourself dressed. I've ordered a table."

The dining room was crowded, but a corner table had been
reserved for them and laid for a crayfish dinner. On each of their
plates lay a paper hat and a bib, and each of the bibs had a

verse printed in red across it. They sat down and Martin Beck looked dismally at his hat, made of blue crepe paper, with a shiny paper visor and POLICE in gold letters above the visor.

The crayfish were delicious, and the men did not talk much as they ate. When they had finished them, Kollberg was still hungry—an almost permanent state of affairs—so he ordered a steak fillet. While they waited for it, he said:

"There were four guys and a broad together with him that night before he left. I made a list for you. It's up in my room."

"Good," said Martin Beck. "Was it difficult?"

"Not especially. I got some help from Melander."

"Melander, yes. What's the time?"

"Half past nine."

Martin Beck got up and left Kollberg alone with his steak. Of course, Melander had already gone to bed and Martin Beck waited patiently through several rings before the telephone was answered.

"Were you asleep in bed?"

"Yes, but it doesn't matter. Are you back?"

"In Malmö. How did things go with Alf Matsson?"

"I found out what you asked me to. Do you want to know now?"

"Yes, please."

"Wait a moment."

Melander went away, but returned very shortly.

"I wrote a report, but it's still at the office. Perhaps I can tell you from memory," he said.

"I'm sure you can," said Martin Beck.

"It deals with Thursday, the twenty-first of July. In the morning Alf Matsson first went up to the magazine, where he picked up his tickets from the office and four hundred kronor from the cash desk. Then he left almost at once and collected his passport and visa from the Hungarian Embassy. After that, he went back to Fleminggatan and, I imagine, packed his suitcase. Anyhow, he changed clothes. In the morning he had been wearing gray trousers, a gray jersey sweater, a blue machine-knit blazer with no lapels and beige suede shoes. In the afternoon and evening, he was wearing a lead-gray suit of thin flannel, a white shirt, black knit tie, black shoes and a gray-beige poplin coat."

It was warm in the phone booth. Martin Beck had got a piece of paper out of his pocket and was scribbling down some notes as Melander was talking.

"Yes, go on," he said.

"At quarter past twelve, he took a taxi from Fleminggatan to the Tankard, where he had lunch with Sven-Erik Molin, Per Kronkvist and Pia Bolt. Her name's Ingrid, but she's called Pia. He drank several steins of beer during and after the meal. At three o'clock, Pia Bolt left and the three men stayed on. About an hour later that is, about four o'clock—Stig Lund and Åke Gunnarsson came in and sat down at their table. They went over to drinking whisky then. Alf Matsson drank whisky and water. The conversation at the table was shop talk, but the waitress remembers that Alf Matsson said he was going away. Where to, she didn't hear."

"Was he drunk?" said Martin Beck.

"Must have been a little, but not noticeably. Not then. Can you hang on a moment?"

Melander went away again and Martin Beck opened the door of the telephone booth wide to let in a little air while he waited. Then Melander came back.

"Just getting my dressing gown on. Where was I? Yes, of course, at the Tankard. At six o'clock, they left—that's Kronkvist, Lund, Gunnarsson, Molin and Matsson—and took a taxi to the Golden Peace and had dinner and drinks. The conversation was mostly about various mutual acquaintances and liquor and girls. Alf Matsson was beginning to get very high and made loud comments about female guests there. Among other things, he's said to have shouted to a middle-aged woman artist, who was sitting at the other side of the room, something like, "Stunning pair of tits you've got there. Can I rest my head on them?" At half past nine they all moved on to the Opera

House bar by taxi. There, they went on drinking whisky. Alf Matsson was drinking whisky and soda. Pia Bolt, who was already at the Opera House bar, joined Matsson and the other four men. At about midnight, Kronkvist and Lund left the restaurant, and shortly before one, Pia Bolt left with Molin. They were all drunk. Matsson and Gunnarsson stayed until the place closed and they were both very drunk. Matsson could not walk straight and accosted several women. I haven't managed to find out what happened after that, but presume he went home in a taxi."

"Didn't anyone notice when he left?"

"No, no one I talked to. Most of the guests leaving at that time were more or less drunk, and the staff were in a hurry to get home."

"Thanks a lot," said Martin Beck. "Will you do me another favor? Go up to Matsson's flat early tomorrow morning and see if you can find that lead-gray suit he was wearing that evening."

"Didn't you go there?" said Melander. "Before you went to Hungary?"

"Yes," said Martin Beck, "but I haven't got the memory of an elephant, like you. Go to bed and sleep now. I'll phone you tomorrow morning."

He returned to Kollberg, who had already polished off the steak and a dessert which had left sticky pink traces behind it on the plate in front of him.

"Had he found anything?"

"I don't know," said Martin Beck. "Perhaps."

They had coffee and Martin Beck told Kollberg about Budapest and Szluka and about Ari Boeck and her German friends. Then they took the elevator up and Martin Beck fetched Kollberg's typed report before going to bed.

He undressed, switched on the bed lamp and turned out the overhead light. Then he got into bed and began to read.

Ingrid (Pia) Bolt, born 1939 in Norrköping, unmarried, secretary, own flat at Strindbergsgatan 51.

Is included in the same gang as Matsson, but doesn't like

M. much and has probably never had relations with him. Has gone around with Stig Lund for a year until quite recently. Nowadays seems to go around with Molin. Secretary at a fashion firm, Studio 45.

Per Kronkvist, born 1936 in Luleå, divorced, reporter on evening paper. Shares a flat with Lund, Sveavägen 88.

One of the gang, but no great friend of Matsson's. Divorced in 1936 in Luleå, since then a resident in Stockholm. Drinks quite a bit, nervous and restless. Appears stupid, but a nice guy. Found guilty of drunken driving in May 1965.

Stig Lund, born 1932 in Gothenburg, unmarried, photographer on the same magazine as Kronkvist. Flat on Sveavägen owned by the magazine.

Came to Stockholm in 1960 and has known Matsson since that time. They spent a lot of time together earlier, but during the last two years they have only met because they go to the same pubs. Quiet and gentle, drinks a lot and usually falls asleep at the table when he's drunk. Ex-athlete, took part in competitions with cross-country running his specialty, 1945–51.

Åke Gunnarsson, born 1932 in Jakobstad, Finland. Unmarried, journalist, writes about cars. Own flat, Svartensgatan 6.

Came to Sweden 1950. Journalist on various auto magazines and in the daily press since 1959. Earlier various jobs such as auto mechanic. Speaks Swedish almost without accent. Moved to flat on Svartensgatan July 1 of this year; before that he lived in Hagalund. Plans to marry at beginning of September, to a girl from Uppsala who is not one of the gang. No more friendly with Matsson than the aforementioned. Drinks quite a bit, but is known for not appearing drunk when he is. Seems quite a bright boy.

Sven-Erik Molin, born 1933 in Stockholm, divorced, journalist, house in Enskede.

Alf Matsson's "best friend," i.e. he maintains he is, but speaks ill of M. behind his back. Divorced in Stockholm four years ago, keeps up support payments and sees his children now and again. Conceited, overbearing and tough attitude, especially when drunk, which happens often. Charged with intoxication in Stockholm twice, 1963 and 1965. Relationship with Pia Bolt not very serious on his side.

There are some more in the group: Krister Sjöberg, com-

mercial artist; Bror Forsgren, advertising representative; Lena
Rosén, journalist; Bengtsfors, journalist; Jack Meredith, film
cameraman, as well as a few more, more or less peripheral.
None of these was actually present on the day or evening
in question.

Martin Beck got up and fetched the piece of paper he had
made notes on while talking to Melander.

He took the paper back to bed with him.

Before putting out the light, he read the whole lot through
again—Kollberg's report and his own carelessly scribbled notes.

26

Saturday, the thirteenth of August, was gray and
windy, and the plane to Stockholm took its time against the
headwind.

The lingering taste of crayfish was anything but delicious at
this time of day and the paper mug of bad coffee that the airline had to offer hardly improved matters. Martin Beck leaned
his head against the vibrating window and watched the clouds.

After a while he tried smoking, but it tasted disgusting. Kollberg was reading a daily from southern Sweden, glancing critically at the cigarette. He probably did not feel too good either.

As far as Alf Matsson was concerned, it could now be said
that he was probably seen for the last time exactly three weeks
ago—in the foyer of the Hotel Duna in Budapest.

The pilot informed them that the weather was cloudy and
that the temperature was fifteen degrees centigrade in Stockholm, and it was drizzling.

Martin Beck extinguished his cigarette in the ashtray and
said, "That murder you were on ten days ago, is it cleared up?"

"Oh, yes."

"No difficulties?"

"No. Psychologically, it was utterly uninteresting, if that's what you mean. Drunk as pigs, both of them. The guy who lived in the flat sat there giving the other guy trouble until he got angry and hit him with a bottle. Then he got scared and hit him twenty times more. But you know all that."

"And afterward. Did he try to get away?"

"Oh, yes, of course. He went home and wrapped up his bloodstained clothes. Then he got a bottle of wood alcohol and went and sat under Skanstull Bridge. All we had to do was to go and pick him up. Then he flatly denied everything for a while and then began to bawl."

After a brief pause, he said, still without looking up, "He's got a screw or two missing. Skanstull Bridge! But he did his best."

Kollberg lowered his paper and looked at Martin Beck.

"Exactly," he said. "He did his best."

He returned to his paper.

Martin Beck frowned, picked up the list he had received the night before and read it through again. Time and time again, until they arrived. He put the paper in his pocket and fastened his safety belt. Then came the usual few minutes of unpleasantness as the plane waddled in the wind and slid down its invisible chute. Gardens and rooftops and two bounces on the concrete, and then he could let out his breath again.

They exchanged a few remarks in the domestic flight lounge while they were waiting for their luggage.

"Are you going out to the island tonight?"

"No, I'll wait a bit."

"There's something rotten about this Matsson story."

"Yes."

"Aggravating."

In the middle of Traneberg Bridge, Kollberg said, "And it's even more aggravating that we can't stop thinking about the miserable business. Matsson was a boor. If he's really disappeared, then that's a good deed done. If he's on the run, then someone'll get him one of these days. That's not our business.

And if by any chance he's somehow died down there, then that's nothing to do with us either. Is it?"

"That's right."

"But supposing the man just goes on having disappeared. Then we'll be thinking about it for ten years. Christ!"

"You're not being particularly logical."

"No. Exactly," said Kollberg.

The police station seemed unusually quiet, but of course it was Saturday and, despite everything, still summer. On Martin Beck's desk lay a number of uninteresting letters and a note from Melander:

"A pair of black shoes in the flat. Old. Not used for a long time. No dark-gray suit."

Outside the window, the wind tore at the treetops and the rain was driving against the windowpane. He thought of the Danube and the steamers and the breeze from the sunny hills. Viennese waltzes. The soft, warm night air. The bridge. The quay. Martin Beck gingerly felt the bump on the back of his head with his fingers, then went back to his desk and sat down.

Kollberg came in, looked at Melander's message, scratched his stomach and said, "It's probably our concern in any case."

"Yes, I think so."

Martin Beck thought for a moment.

"When you were in Rumania, did you turn in your passport?"

"Yes, the police collected your passport at the airport. Then you got it back at the hotel a week later. I saw mine standing in my pigeonhole for several days before they gave it to me. It was a big hotel. The police handed in whole bundles of passports every evening."

Martin Beck pulled the telephone toward him.

"Budapest 298-317, a person-to-person call to Major Vilmos Szluka. Yes, Major s-z-l-u-k-a. No, it's in Hungary."

He returned to the window and stared out into the rain without saying anything. Kollberg sat in the visitor's chair and studied his nails. Neither of them moved or spoke until the telephone rang.

Someone said in very bad German, "Yes, Major Szluka will come in a minute."

Steps echoed through police headquarters in Deák Ferenc Tér. Then Szluka's voice came over: "Good morning. How are things in Stockholm?"

"It's raining and windy. Cold."

"Oh, it's over 85° Fahrenheit here. Almost too hot. I was just thinking of going to Palatino. Anything new?"

"Not yet."

"Same here. We haven't found him yet. Can I help you with anything?"

"Doesn't it sometimes happen that people lose their passports now during the tourist season?"

"Yes, unfortunately. It's always troublesome. Fortunately that's not one of my concerns."

"Could you find out whether any foreigner has reported the loss of his passport at the Ifjuság or the Duna since the twenty-first of July?"

"Of course. But it's not my department, as I said. Will it be all right if I get the answer back by five?"

"You can telephone whenever you like. And one more thing."

"Yes?"

"If someone has reported this, do you think you could find out what the person looked like? Just a brief description."

"I'll call you at five o'clock. Good-bye."

"Good-bye. Hope you don't miss going to the baths."

He put down the receiver. Kollberg looked at him suspiciously.

"What the hell is the business about baths?"

"A sulfur bath, where you sit in marble armchairs under water."

"Oh."

There was a brief silence. Kollberg scratched his head and said, "So in Budapest he was wearing a blue blazer and gray trousers and brown shoes."

"Yes, and the raincoat."

"And in his suitcase there was a blue blazer."

"Yes."

"And a pair of gray trousers."

"Yes."

"And a pair of brown shoes."

"Yes."

"And the night before he left he was wearing a dark suit and black shoes."

"Yes, and the raincoat."

"And neither the shoes nor the suit are in his flat."

"No."

"Christ!" said Kollberg simply.

"Yes."

The atmosphere in the room changed and seemed to become less tense. Martin Beck rummaged in his drawer, found a dry old Florida and lit it. Like the man in Malmö, he was trying to give up smoking, but much more halfheartedly.

Kollberg yawned and looked at his watch.

"Shall we go and eat somewhere?"

"Yes, why not?"

"The Tankard?"

"Sure."

27

The wind had dropped and in Vasa Park the light rain was falling peacefully down onto the double row of tombola stalls, a carousel and two policemen in black rain capes. The carousel was running and on one of the painted horses sat a lone child: a little girl in a red-plastic coat with a hood. She was riding round and round in the rain with a solemn expression on her face and her eyes focused straight ahead. Her parents were standing under an umbrella a little way away, regarding the amusement park with melancholy eyes. A fresh smell of greenery and wet leaves came from the park. It was Saturday afternoon and, despite everything, still summer.

The restaurant diagonally opposite the park was almost empty. The only audible sound in the place was a faint comforting rustle from the evening papers of two elderly regular customers and the muted sound of darts thudding into the board in the dart room. Martin Beck and Kollberg took a seat in the bar, six feet or so from the table that was the favorite refuge of Alf Matsson and his fellow journalists. There was no one there now, but in the middle of the table stood a glass containing a red reservation card. Presumably this was a fixture.

"The lunch hour is over now," said Kollberg. "In an hour or so people begin dropping in again, and in the evening it's so chock-full of people spilling beer all over each other that you can hardly get your foot inside."

The atmosphere did not make for extensive discussion. They ate a late lunch in silence. Outside the Swedish summer was pouring away. Kollberg drained a stein of beer, folded up his table napkin, wiped his mouth and said, "Is it difficult to get across the border down there? Without a passport?"

"Fairly. They say the borders are guarded well. A foreigner who didn't know his way around would hardly make it."

"And if you leave by the ordinary routes, then you have to have a visa in your passport?"

"Yes, and an exit permit besides. That's a loose piece of paper that you get on entry and keep in your passport until you leave the country. Then the passport control people take it. The police also stamp the date of departure beside the visa in your passport. Look."

Martin Beck took his passport out of his inside pocket and put it on the table. Kollberg studied the stamps. Then he said:

"And assuming that you've got both a visa and an exit permit, then you can cross any border you like?"

"Yes. You have five countries to choose from—Czechoslovakia, the Soviet Union, Rumania, Yugoslavia and Austria. And you can go any way you like—by air, train, car or boat."

"Boat? From Hungary?"

"Yes, on the Danube. From Budapest you can get to Vienna or Bratislava in a few hours by hydrofoil."

"And you can ride a bicycle, walk, swim, ride horseback or crawl?" said Kollberg.

"Yes, as long as you make your way to a border station."

"And you can go to Austria and Yugoslavia without a visa?"

"That depends on what kind of passport you've got. If it's Swedish for instance, or German or Italian, then you don't need one. On a Hungarian passport you can go to Czechoslovakia or Yugoslavia without a visa."

"But it's hardly likely that he did that?"

"No."

They went on to coffee. Kollberg was still looking at the stamps in the passport.

"The Danes didn't stamp it when you got to Kastrup," he said.

"No."

"Then in other words there's no evidence that you've returned to Sweden."

"No," said Martin Beck.

A moment later he added, "But on the other hand, I'm sitting here—right?"

A number of customers had dropped in during the last half hour, and there was already a shortage of tables. A man of about thirty-five came in and sat down at the table with the red reservation card on it, was given a stein of beer and sat leafing through the evening paper, seemingly bored. Now and again he looked anxiously toward the door, as if he were waiting for someone. He had a beard and was wearing thick-rimmed glasses, a brown checked tweed jacket, a white shirt, brown trousers and black shoes.

"Who's that?" said Martin Beck.

"Don't know. They all look alike. Besides, there are a number of marginal creatures who only show up now and then."

"It's not Molin, anyhow, because I'd recognize him."

Kollberg glanced at the man.

"Gunnarsson maybe."

Martin Beck thought.

"No, I've seen him too."

A woman came in. She had red hair and was quite young, dressed in a brick-red sweater, tweed skirt and green stockings. She moved easily, letting her eyes wander over the room as she fingered her nose. She sat down at the table with the red card and said, "Ciao, Per."

"Ciao, sweetheart."

"Per," said Kollberg. "That's Kronkvist. And that's Pia Bolt."

"Why have they all got beards?"

Martin Beck said it thoughtfully, as if he had pondered the problem for a long time.

"Perhaps they're false," said Kollberg solemnly.

He looked at his watch.

"Just to give us trouble," he said.

"We'd better get back," said Martin Beck. "Did you tell Stenström to come on up?"

Kollberg nodded. As they were leaving, they heard the man named Per Kronkvist call out to the waitress:

"More beer! Over here!"

It was very quiet at the police station. Stenström was sitting in the downstairs office playing patience.

Kollberg looked critically at him, and said, "Have you already started with that? What are you going to do when you get old?"

"Sit thinking the same thing I'm thinking now: why am I sitting here?"

"You're going to check some alibis," said Martin Beck. "Give him the list, Lennart."

Stenström was given the list. He glanced at it.

"Now?"

"Yes, this evening."

"Molin, Lund, Kronkvist, Gunnarsson, Bengtsfors, Pia Bolt. Who is Bengtsfors?"

"That's a mistake," said Kollberg gloomily. "Supposed to be Bengt Fors. The *t* on my typewriter sticks to the *s*."

"Shall I question the girl too?"

"Yes, if it amuses you," said Martin Beck. "She's at the Tankard."

"Can I talk to them direct?"

"Why not? Routine investigation in the Alf Matsson case. Everyone knows what it's all about now. How's things with the Narcotics boys, by the way?"

"I spoke to Jacobsson," said Stenström. "They'll soon have it all tied up. As soon as the heads here knew that Matsson had had it, they began to talk. I was thinking of something, by the way. Matsson sold the stuff directly to a few people who were really desperate and he made them pay through the nose."

"What were you thinking?"

"Couldn't it be one of the poor devils he skinned—that one of his customers got tired of him, so to speak?"

"Could be," said Martin Beck solemnly.

"Especially at the movies," said Kollberg. "In America."

Stenström put the piece of paper into his pocket and got up. At the door he stopped and said huffily, "Sometimes something different actually might happen here too."

"Possibly," said Kollberg. "But you've forgotten that Matsson disappeared in Hungary, on his way to pick up some more stuff for his poor customers. Now scram."

Stenström left.

"That was nasty of you," said Martin Beck.

"He might do a little thinking for himself too," said Kollberg.

"That's what he was doing."

"Huh!"

Martin Beck went out into the corridor. Stenström was just putting on his coat.

"Look at their passports."

Stenström nodded.

"Don't go alone."

"Are they dangerous?" said Stenström sarcastically.

"Routine," said Martin Beck.

He went back in to Kollberg. They sat in silence until the telephone rang. Martin picked up the receiver.

"Your call to Budapest will be coming through at seven o'clock instead of five," said the telephone operator.

They digested the message for a moment. Then Kollberg said, "God. This is no fun."

"No," said Martin Beck. "It's not much fun."

"Two hours," said Kollberg. "Shall we drive around a little and have a look-see?"

"Yes, why not?"

They drove over West Bridge. The Saturday traffic had thinned out and the bridge was practically deserted. On the crest they passed a German tourist coach that had slowed down. Martin Beck saw the passengers inside standing up and staring out across the silvery bay and at the misty silhouette of the city.

"Molin is the only one who lives outside the city," said Kollberg. "Let's take him first."

They went on over Liljeholm Bridge, and Kollberg swung in off the main road among the houses, twisting along the narrow roads for a while, before finding the right house. He let the car run slowly past the row of hedges and fences as he read the names on the gateposts.

"Here it is," he said. "Molin lives on the left. That's his porch you can see. The house must have been occupied once by a single family, but now it's divided. The other entrance is around the back."

"Who lives in the other part of the house?" said Martin Beck.

"A retired customs official and his wife."

The garden in front of the house was wild, with gnarled apple trees and overgrown berrybushes. But the hedges around it were well trimmed, and the white fencing looked recently painted.

"Big garden," said Kollberg. "And well sheltered. Do you want to see any more?"

"No. Drive on."

"Then we'll take Svartensgatan," said Kollberg. "Gunnarsson."

They drove back into the south side of the city, parking the car in Mosebacke Square.

Svartensgatan 6 was right by the square. It was an old building with a large paved courtyard. Gunnarsson lived three floors up, facing the street.

"He hasn't lived here all that long," said Martin Beck when they had got back to the car.

"Since the first of July."

"And before that he lived in Hagalund. Do you know where?"

Kollberg stopped at a red traffic light.

He nodded toward the large corner window of the Opera House bar.

"Perhaps they're all sitting together in there now," he said. "All of them except Matsson. In Hagalund? Yes, I've got the address."

"Then we'll go there later," said Martin Beck. "Go along Strandvägen. I'd like to look at the boats."

They drove along Strandvägen and Martin Beck looked at the boats. At one quay lay a large white ocean-going vessel with the American flag aft, and farther on, flanked by two Åland sailing-smacks, lay a Polish motor launch.

Outside the entrance of the building where Pia Bolt lived on Strindbergsgatan, a small boy in a checked sou'wester and poncho was pushing a plastic double-decker bus back and forth across the step as he imitated the sound of its motor with his lips. The sound grew muted and uneven as he braked the bus to allow Kollberg and Martin Beck to pass.

Inside the entrance, Stenström was standing gloomily looking at Kollberg's list.

"What are you hanging around here for?" said Kollberg.

"She's not home. And she wasn't at the Tankard. I was just wondering where to go next. But if you're thinking of taking over, then I can go home."

"Try the Opera House bar," said Kollberg.

"Why are you on your own, by the way," said Martin Beck.

"I've had Rönn with me. He'll be back in a minute. He's just gone home to his old lady with some flowers. It's her birthday and she lives right here on the corner."

"How's it going?" said Martin Beck.

"We've checked Lund and Kronkvist. They left the Opera House bar about midnight and went straight to the Hamburger Exchange. There they met two gals they knew, and at about three they went back home with one of them."

He looked at the list.

"Her name is Svensson and she lives in Lidingö. They stayed there until eight o'clock on Friday morning and then took a taxi together to work. At one o'clock, they went to the Tankard and sat there until five, when they went to Karlstad on a reporting job. I haven't got around to the others yet."

"I realize that," said Martin Beck. "Just carry on. We'll be at the station after seven. Phone if you've finished before too late."

The rain grew heavier as they drove toward Hagalund. When Kollberg stopped the car outside the low block of flats in which Gunnarsson had lived until two months ago, the water was pouring down the windowpanes and the drumming on the car roof was deafening.

They put up their coatcollars and ran across the pavement into the entrance. The building was three-storied and on one of the doors on the second floor there was a calling card fastened on with a thumbtack. The name on the calling card was also on the list of tenants in the entrance hall, and the white plastic letters looked newer and whiter than the others.

They walked back to the car and drove around the block, then stopped in front of the building. The flat where Gunnarsson had presumably lived had only two windows and appeared to consist of only one room.

"It must be a pretty small flat," said Kollberg. "He's going to get married now since he's got a bigger one."

Martin Beck looked out into the rain. He wanted to smoke

and felt cold. There was a field and wooded slope on the other side of the street. At the far end of the field was a newly built highrise building and another one was in the process of being built beside it. The whole field was probably going to be built on with a row of identical highrises. From the dismal block where Gunnarsson had lived, one at least had an open, country-like view, but now that, too, would be spoiled.

In the middle of the field stood the charred remains of a burnt-out house.

"A fire?" he said, pointing.

Kollberg leaned forward and peered through the rain.

"That's an old farm," he said. "I remember seeing it last summer. A fine old wooden house, but no one lived there. I think the fire department burned it down. You know—to practice. They set it alight and then put the fire out, and then they set it alight again and put it out again, and they go on like that until there's nothing left. Pity with such a fine old place. But they probably need the land to build on."

He looked at his watch and started the engine.

"We'll have to step on it if we're going to get your call," he said.

The rain poured down the windshield and Kollberg had to drive carefully. They sat in silence all the way back. When they got out of the car it was five to seven and already dark.

The telephone rang so precisely on the dot of seven that it seemed almost unnatural. It was unnatural.

"Where the hell's Lennart?" said Kollberg's wife.

Martin Beck handed over the receiver and tried not to listen to Kollberg's replies in the dialogue that followed.

"Yes, I'm coming soon now. . . . Yes, in a little while, I said. . . . Tomorrow? That'll be hard, I expect. . . ."

Martin Beck retired to the bathroom and did not come back until he had heard the receiver being replaced

"We should have children," said Kollberg. "Poor thing, sitting out there on her own, waiting for me."

They had only been married six months, so things would probably work out all right.

A bit later the call came through.

"I'm sorry to have kept you waiting," said Szluka. "It's more difficult to get hold of people here on Saturday. However, you were right."

"About the passport?"

"Yes. A Belgian student lost his passport at Hotel Ifjúság."

"When?"

"That hasn't been determined at the moment. He came to the hotel on Friday the twenty-second of July in the afternoon. Alf Matsson came in the evening of the same day."

"So it fits."

"Yes, it does, doesn't it? The difficulty is this. This man, whose name is Roeder, is visiting Hungary for the first time and doesn't know the regulations here. He himself claims that he found it quite natural to hand in his passport and not get it back until he had left the hotel. As he was to stay for three weeks, he didn't give the matter a thought and did not ask for his passport before Monday, in other words the day we met for the first time. He needed it to apply for a visa to Bulgaria. All this is, of course, according to the man's own statement."

"It could be right."

"Yes, of course. At the hotel reception they at once said that Roeder had been given back his passport on the morning after he had arrived, that is, the twenty-third, or the same day Matsson moved to Hotel Duna—and disappeared. Roeder swears he was never given his passport, and the hotel staff are equally certain his passport was put in his pigeonhole on the Friday evening and that, consequently, he should have received it back when he came down on the Saturday morning. That's the routine."

"Does anyone remember that he actually received it?"

"No. But that would be too much to ask. At this time of year, it often happens that people at the reception desk receive up to fifty foreign passports a day and hand out the same number. Also, the people who sort the passports into the pigeonholes are not the same ones who hand them out the next morning.

"Have you seen this Roeder?"

"Yes, he's still staying at the hotel. His embassy is arranging for his journey home."

"And? I mean, does it fit?"

"He has a beard. Otherwise they aren't especially alike, judging from the pictures. But unfortunately people don't often look like their passport photos either. Someone could well have stolen the passport out of the pigeonhole during the night. Nothing could be simpler. The night porter is alone and naturally has to turn his back sometimes, or leave his place. And the officials who check passports haven't time to study faces when tourists are pouring back and forth across the border. If we work on the theory that your fellow countryman took Roeder's passport, then he might well have left the country with its help."

There was a short silence. Then Szluka said:

"Someone has done it, anyway."

Martin Beck sat up.

"Do you know that?"

"Yes. We heard about it twenty minutes ago. Roeder's exit permit is in our files. It was handed in to the border police in Hegyeshalom on the afternoon of Saturday the twenty-third of July. One of the passengers on the Budapest–Vienna express. And that passenger can't have been Roeder as he's still here."

Szluka paused again. Then he said hesitantly, "I suppose this means that Matsson has left Hungary."

"No," said Martin Beck. "He's never been there at all."

28

Martin Beck slept badly and got up early. The flat in Bagarmossen was dismal and lifeless and the familiar objects seemed irrelevant and dreary. He took a shower. Shaved. Took out his newly pressed gray suit. Dressed carefully and correctly.

Then went out on to the balcony. It had stopped raining. He looked at the thermometer. It was 60° Fahrenheit. He got himself a lugubrious grass-widower's breakfast of tea and rusks. Then he sat down and waited.

Kollberg came at nine o'clock. He had Stenström with him in the car. They drove to the police station.

"How did it go?" said Martin Beck.

"So so," said Stenström.

He leafed through his notebook.

"Molin was working on that Saturday, that's clear. He was at the office from eight o'clock in the morning. On that Friday, he seems to have been at home sleeping off his hangover. We argued a bit over his being asleep. He said that he hadn't been sleeping, but had passed out. 'Don't you know what it is to pass out and have little demons sitting there on your pillow, copper? That's good. Then you're suited to being a policeman, because you don't understand a god damn about anything.' I wrote down that remark, word for word."

"Why did he have little demons?" said Kollberg.

"That didn't come out. Didn't seem to know himself, and what he'd done the night between Thursday and Friday, he couldn't remember. He said he was grateful for that. He was pretty darned insolent and awkward all around."

"Go on," said Martin Beck.

"Well, I'm afraid I was wrong yesterday when I said Lund and Kronkvist were clear. It turned out, in fact, that it wasn't Kronkvist but Fors who had gone with those girls to Lidingö. On the other hand, it was Kronkvist who went with Lund to Karlstad, not on Friday but on Saturday. It is a bit of a mix-up, all this, but I don't think Lund was lying when he made the first statement. He really didn't remember. He and Kronkvist seem to have been the most drunk of the lot of them. Lund got everything mixed up. Fors was brighter and when I got hold of him things became clearer. Lund collapsed as soon as they got to the girls' place, and they didn't get a sign of life out of him all that Friday. Then on Saturday morning, he rang up Fors, who went there and picked him up, and then they went to the pub, not to the Tankard, as Lund had thought, but to the Opera House bar. When Lund had had something to eat and a couple of beers, he revived and went home and picked up Kronkvist and all his photographic gear. Kronkvist was at home at that time."

"What had he done before that?"

"Lain at home feeling ill and lonely, he said. The only definite thing is that he was there at half past four on Saturday afternoon."

"Is that verified?"

"Yes, they got to the hotel in Karlstad in the evening. Kronkvist also had a fearful hangover, he said. Lund said he was too high to have anything. Lund hasn't got a beard, by the way. I made a note of that."

"Uh-huh."

"Then there was Gunnarsson. His memory was a little better. He sat at home writing on Friday. On Saturday he was at the office at first in the morning and then in the evening, turning in various articles."

"Are you certain?"

"I wouldn't say that. The office there is large and I couldn't find anyone who could remember anything special. On the other hand, it's true that he handed in an article, but that could just as well have been in the evening as in the morning."

"And passports?"

"Wait a minute. Pia Bolt was also quite explicit. She refused to say where she'd been on that Thursday night, however. I got the impression that she'd been sleeping with someone but didn't want to say who."

"Sounds possible," said Kollberg. "It was Thursday and all that."

"What do you mean by that?" said Stenström.

"Nothing. Perhaps that was a little below the belt."

"Go on," said Martin Beck.

"On Saturday, anyway, she was at home with her mother from eleven in the morning on. I checked that in a discreet way.

It was true. Well, now there are the passports. Molin refused to show his. He didn't have to identify himself in his own home, he said. Lund had an almost new passport. The last stamp was from Arlanda on the sixteenth of June, when he returned from Israel. That seemed to be all right."

"Refused to show his passport!" said Kollberg. "And you let him."

"Pia Bolt had been to Majorca for a week two years ago, that is all. Kronkvist had an old passport. It looked a mess, covered with notes and scribbles. The last stamp from Gothenburg in May. Returning from England. Gunnarsson also had an old passport, almost full, but a bit cleaner. He has stamps from Arlanda, left the country on the seventh of May and re-entered the tenth. Had been to the Renault factories in Billancourt, he said. Evidently they don't stamp passports in France."

"No, that's right," said Martin Beck.

"Then there were the others. I haven't had time to get around to them all. Krister Sjöberg was at home with his family in Älvsjö. That Meredith, he's an American—colored, by the way."

"We'll skip that," said Kollberg. "We couldn't take him in anyhow, or we'd be lynched by the Mods."

"Now you're being really stupid."

"I usually am. Anyhow, I don't think you need go on."

"No, I don't think so," said Martin Beck.

"Do you know who it is?" said Stenström.

"We think so at least."

"Who?"

Kollberg glared at Stenström.

"Think for yourself, man," he said. "In the first place, was it Alf Matsson who was in Budapest? Would Matsson take a small fortune to pay for drugs and then not bother about it and leave the money in his bag at the hotel? Would Matsson throw his key down outside the entrance of the police station? A man who ought to make a long detour around any policeman he ever saw down there? Why should Matsson disappear of his own free will, in such an improvised manner?"

"No, of course not."

"Why should Matsson travel to Hungary dressed in a blue blazer, gray trousers and suede shoes, when he had exactly the same kind of clothes packed in his bag? What happened to Matsson's dark suit? The one he had on the night before and which was not in his bag and is not in his flat?"

"O.K. It wasn't Matsson. Who was it then?"

"Someone who had Matsson's glasses and raincoat, someone with a beard. Who was last seen with Matsson? Who had no alibi whatsoever before Saturday evening, at the earliest? Who of all that lot was sufficiently sober and intelligent to be able to cook up this little story? Think it over."

Stenström looked very solemn.

"I've thought of something else," said Kollberg.

He spread the map of Budapest out on the table.

"Look here. There's the hotel and there's the central station, or whatever it's called."

"Budapest Nyugati."

"Maybe. If I was going to walk from the hotel to the station, I would walk this way and thus pass police headquarters."

"That's right, but in that case you'd go to the wrong station. The trains to Vienna go from down here, from the old Eastern Railway Station."

Kollberg said nothing. He went on staring at the map.

Martin Beck spread out a blueprint of the Solna area and nodded at Stenström.

"Go on out to the Solna police," he said. "Ask them to rope this area off. There's a burnt-out house there. We'll be there soon."

"Now, at once?"

"Yes."

Stenström left. Martin Beck hunted for a cigarette and lit it. He smoked in silence. And looked at Kollberg who was sitting quite still. Then he put out the cigarette and said, "Let's go, then."

Kollberg drove swiftly through the empty Sunday streets and then they crossed the bridge. The sun came out from behind driving clouds and a light breeze swept across the water. Martin Beck looked absently at a group of small sailing boats which were just rounding a buoy in the bay.

They drove in silence and parked in the same place as the day before. Kollberg pointed at a black Lancia parked a little farther on.

"That's his car," he said. "Then he's probably at home."

They crossed Svartensgatan and pushed open the door. The air felt raw and damp. They walked in silence up the worn stairs to the fifth floor.

29

The door was opened immediately.

The man in the doorway was wearing a dressing gown and slippers, and looking extremely surprised.

"Sorry," he said. "I thought you were my fiancée."

Martin Beck recognized him at once. It was the same man Molin had pointed out to him at the Tankard, the day before his Budapest trip. An open, pleasant face. Calm blue eyes. Quite powerfully built. He had a beard and was of medium height, but this was—as in the case of the Belgian student, Roeder—the only resemblance to Matsson.

"We're from the police. My name is Beck. This is Inspector Kollberg."

The introductions were stiff and courteous.

"Kollberg."

"Gunnarsson."

"May we come in for a minute?" said Martin Beck.

"Of course. What's it about?"

"We would like to talk about Alf Matsson."

"A policeman came yesterday and asked me about the same thing."

"Yes, we know that."

As Martin Beck and Kollberg entered the flat, they underwent a change. It happened to them both at the same time and without either of them being aware of it. All that had been tense, uncertain and vigilant about them vanished and was replaced by a routine calm, a mechanical determination which showed that they knew what was going to happen and that they had been through the same thing before.

They walked through the flat without saying anything. It was light and spacious and furnished with care and consideration, but in some way gave the impression that it had not yet been lived in properly. Much of the furniture was new and still looked as if it were standing in a shop window.

Two of the rooms had windows facing the street and the bedroom and kitchen looked out over the courtyard. The door to the bathroom was open and the light was on inside. Evidently the man had just begun getting washed and dressed when they had rung the bell. In the bedroom there were two wide beds standing close together, and one had recently been slept in. On the bedside table by the unmade bed stood a half-empty bottle of mineral water, a glass, two pillboxes and a framed photograph. There was also a rocking chair in the room, two stools, and a dressing table with drawers and movable mirror. The photo was of a young woman. She had fair hair, clean, healthy features and very light-colored eyes. No makeup, but a silver chain around her neck, a so-called Bismarck chain. Martin Beck recognized the kind. Sixteen years ago he had given his wife an exact replica of it. They went back into the study. The tour was complete.

"Do please sit down," said Gunnarsson.

Martin Beck nodded and sat down in one of the basket chairs by the desk, which was clearly intended for two people. The man in the dressing gown remained standing and glanced at Kollberg, who was still moving round the flat.

Manuscripts, books and papers lay in neat piles on the table. A page already started was inserted into the typewriter, and beside the telephone stood yet another framed photograph.

Martin Beck at once recognized the woman with the silver chain and light eyes. But this picture had been taken out-of-doors. Her head was thrown back and she was laughing at the photographer, the wind tugging at her ruffled fair hair.

"What can I do to help you," said the man in the dressing gown, politely.

Martin Beck looked straight at him. His eyes were still blue and calm and steady. It was quiet in the room. Kollberg could be heard doing something in another part of the flat, presumably in the washroom or the kitchen.

"Tell me what happened," said Martin Beck.

"When?"

"The eve of the twenty-second of July, when you and Matsson left the Opera House bar."

"I've already done that. We parted in the street. I took a taxi and came home. He wasn't going in the same direction and waited for the next one."

Martin Beck leaned his forearms on the desk and looked at the woman in the photograph.

"May I look at your passport?" he said.

The man walked around the desk, sat down and pulled out one of the drawers. The basket chair creaked amiably.

"Here you are," he said.

Martin Beck turned over the pages of the passport. It was old and worn and the last stamp was indeed an entry stamp from Arlanda on the tenth of May. On the next page—which was also the last one in the passport—there were a few notes, among others two telephone numbers and a short verse. The inside of the cover was also full of notes. Most of them seemed to be comments on cars or engines, made long ago and in great haste. The verse was written across on a slant, with a green ball-point pen. He twisted the passport and read:

> There was a young man of Dundee
> Who said "They can't do without me.
> No house is complete
> Without me and my seat.
> My initials are W.C."

The man on the other side of the table followed his glance and explained, "It's a limerick."

"So I see."

"It's about Winston Churchill. They say that he wrote it himself. I heard it on the plane from Paris and thought it was so good that I ought to write it down."

Martin Beck said nothing. He stared at the verse. Underneath the writing, the paper was a little lighter and there were several small green dots that should not have been there. They could have been some perforations from a green stamp on the other side of the page, but no such stamp existed. Stenström ought to have noticed that.

"If you had left the plane in Copenhagen and taken the ferry to Sweden, you'd have been saved the trouble," he said.

"I don't understand what you mean."

The telephone rang. Gunnarsson answered. Kollberg came into the room.

"It's for one of you," said the man in the dressing gown.

Kollberg took the receiver, listened and said, "Oh, yes. Get them going then. Yes, wait out there. We'll be there soon."

He put the receiver down.

"That was Stenström. The fire department burned the house down last Monday."

"We have people searching through the remains of that burnt-out house in Hagalund," said Martin Beck.

"Well, what about it?" said Kollberg.

"I still don't know what you mean."

The man's eyes were still just as steady and open. There was a brief silence, and then Martin Beck shrugged his shoulders and said, "Go in and get dressed."

Without a word, Gunnarsson walked toward the bedroom door. Kollberg followed him.

Martin Beck remained where he was, immobile. His eyes rested again on the photograph. Although actually it was unimportant, for some reason he was annoyed that the conversation should end like this. After having seen the passport, he felt utterly certain, but the idea about the fire department's practice site was a guess, which might very well prove to be wrong. In that case, and if the man managed to maintain his attitude, the investigation would be very troublesome. And yet this was not really the main reason for his dissatisfaction.

Gunnarsson came back five minutes later wearing a gray sweater and brown trousers. He looked at his watch and said, "Now we can go. I'll be having a visitor soon, and would be grateful if . . . "

He smiled and left the sentence unfinished. Martin Beck remained seated.

"We're in no special hurry," he said.

Kollberg came in from the bedroom.

"The trousers and the blue blazer are still hanging in the wardrobe," he said.

Martin Beck nodded. Gunnarsson walked back and forth across the room. He was moving more nervously now, but his expression was as unshakably calm as before.

"Perhaps it's not so bad as it seems," said Kollberg in a friendly way. "You don't have to be so resigned."

Martin Beck glanced at his colleague quickly, then looked at Gunnarsson again. Of course, Kollberg was right. The man had given up. He knew the game was up and he had known it the moment they'd stepped over the threshold. Presumably he was now enveloped in this feeling as if in a cocoon. But still not completely invulnerable. Nevertheless, what had to be done was very unpleasant.

Martin Beck leaned back in the basket chair and waited. Kollberg stood silent and immobile by the bedroom door. Gunnarsson had remained standing in the middle of the floor. He looked at his watch again but said nothing.

A minute went past. Two. Three. The man again looked at his wristwatch. Probably a purely reflex action, and it was clear that it annoyed him. After two minutes more he did it again, but this time tried to mask his maneuver by running the back of his left hand over his face as he glanced down at his wrist. The door of a car slammed somewhere down on the street.

He opened his mouth to say something. Only one word came out.

"If . . ."

Then he was sorry, took two quick steps toward the telephone and said, "Excuse me, I have to call someone."

Martin Beck nodded and looked stubbornly at the telephone. 018. The area code for Uppsala. Everything fitted in. Six figures. Answer on the third ring.

"Hello. This is Åke. Has Ann-Louise left?"

"Oh. When?"

Martin Beck thought he heard a woman's voice say, "About a quarter of an hour ago."

"Oh, yes. Thanks very much. Good-bye."

Gunnarsson replaced the receiver, looked at his watch and said in a light voice, "Well, shall we go now?"

No one replied. Ten long minutes went by. Then Martin Beck said, "Sit down."

The man obeyed very hesitantly. Although he seemed to be making an effort to sit still, the basket chair did not stop creaking. The next time he looked at his watch, Martin Beck saw that his hands were trembling.

Kollberg yawned, much too studiedly or else from nervousness. It was hard to determine which. Two minutes later, the man called Gunnarsson said, "What are we waiting for?"

For the first time there was a trace of uncertainty even in his voice.

Martin Beck looked at him. He said nothing. He wondered what would happen if the man on the other side of the desk suddenly realized that the silence was just as much of a strain on them as it was on him. It probably wouldn't be of much help to him. In some way they were all in the same boat now.

Gunnarsson looked at his watch, picked up a pen that was lying on the desk and at once put it down again in exactly the same place.

Martin Beck looked away and at the photograph, then

glanced at his watch. Twenty minutes had gone by since the phone call. At worst, they had half an hour at their disposal.

He again looked at Gunnarsson and caught himself thinking about everything they had in common. The giant creaking bed. The view. The boats. The room key. The damp heat from the river.

He looked at his watch quite openly. Something about this seemed to irritate the other man considerably—perhaps the reminder that they did in fact have a common interest.

Martin Beck and Kollberg looked at each other for the first time in practically half an hour. If they were right, the end should be very near.

Disintegration came thirty seconds later. Gunnarsson looked from the one man to the other and said in a clear voice, "O.K. What do you want to know?"

No one answered.

"Yes, you're right, of course. It was me."

"What happened?"

"I don't want to talk about it," said the man thickly.

He was staring stubbornly down at the desk now. Kollberg looked at him with a frown, glanced over at Martin Beck and nodded.

Martin Beck drew a deep breath.

"You must realize that we'll find out everything anyhow," he said. "There are witnesses down there who can identify you. We'll find the taxi driver who drove you here that night. He'll remember whether you were alone or not. Your car and flat will be examined by experts. The burnt-out house in Hagalund as well. If a body has been lying there, there'll be enough left of it. That doesn't matter now. Whatever happened to Alf Matsson and wherever he went, we'll find him. You won't be able to hide very much—nothing important, anyway."

Gunnarsson looked straight at him and said, "In that case, I don't understand the point of all this."

Martin Beck knew that he would remember that remark for years, perhaps for the rest of his life.

It was Kollberg who saved the situation. He said tonelessly,

"It is our duty to tell you that you are suspected of manslaughter, or possibly murder. Naturally you have the right to legal representation during the formal hearing."

"Alf came with me in the taxi. We came here. He knew I had a bottle of whisky at home and insisted that we should finish it off."

"And?"

"We had already drunk a good deal. We quarreled."

He fell silent. Shrugged his shoulders.

"I'd rather not talk about it."

"Why did you quarrel?" said Kollberg.

"He . . . he made me mad."

"In what way?"

A swift change in those blue eyes. Uncontrolled and anything but harmless.

"He behaved like a . . . well, he said certain things.

"About my fiancée. Just a moment—I can explain how it started. If you look in the top right-hand drawer . . . there are some photographs there."

Martin Beck pulled out the drawer and found the photographs. He held them carefully between his fingertips. They had been taken on a beach somewhere, and were just the sort of pictures people in love might take on a beach, provided they were quite undisturbed. He went through them swiftly, almost without looking at them. The bottom one was bent and damaged. The woman with the light-colored eyes smiled at the photographer.

"I had been in the bathroom. When I came back, he was standing there rummaging in my drawers. He'd found . . . those pictures. He tried to put one in his pocket. I was already angry with him, but then I became . . . furious."

The man paused briefly and then said apologetically, "Unfortunately I can't remember those particular details very clearly."

Martin Beck nodded.

"I took the photograph away from him, although he resisted.

Then he began shouting filthy things about, well, about Ann-Louise. Of course, I knew that every last word was a lie, but I couldn't bear listening to him. He was talking very loudly. Almost yelling. I think I was afraid the neighbors would wake up too."

The man lowered his eyes again. He looked at his hands and said, "Well, that wasn't all that important. But it probably entered in, I don't know. Do I have to try to repeat . . ."

"Forget the details for the time being," said Kollberg. "What happened?"

Gunnarsson looked stubbornly at his hands.

"I strangled him," he said very quietly.

Martin Beck waited for ten seconds. Then he ran his fore-finger down his nose and said, "And after that?"

"I suddenly turned completely sober, or at least I thought I had. He was lying there on the floor. Dead. It was about two o'clock. Naturally I should have called the police. It didn't seem so simple then."

He thought for a moment.

"Why, everything would have been ruined."

Martin Beck nodded and looked at his watch. This seemed to hurry the other man.

"Well, I sat here probably for a quarter of an hour, roughly, thinking what to do. In this chair. I refused to accept that the situation was hopeless. Everything that had happened was so . . . startling. It seemed so pointless. I wasn't really able to realize that it was me who had suddenly—oh, well, we can talk about that later."

"You knew that Matsson was going to Budapest," said Kollberg.

"Yes, of course. He had his passports and tickets on him. Had only had to go home and pick up his bag. I think it was his glasses that gave me the idea. They had fallen off and were lying here on the floor. They were rather special ones, changing his appearance in some way. Then I happened to think about that house out there. I had sat on the balcony watching the fire department practicing, how they set it alight and extinguished the fire again. Every Monday. They didn't investigate very carefully before setting fire to it. I knew they'd soon completely burn down the little that was left. It's no doubt cheaper than tearing things down in the ordinary way."

Gunnarsson threw a swift, desperate look at Martin Beck and said hastily:

"Then I took his passport, tickets, car keys and the keys to his flat. Then . . ."

He shuddered but collected himself at once.

"Then I carried him down to the car. That was the hardest part, but I was . . . well, I was just about to say I was lucky. I drove out to Hagalund."

"To the old farmhouse?"

"Yes. It was absolutely quiet out there. I carried . . . Alfie up to the attic. It was difficult because the stairs were half gone. And then I put him behind a loose wall, under a mass of rubbish so that no one would find him. He was dead, after all. It didn't matter all that much. I thought."

Martin Beck glanced anxiously at his watch.

"Go on," he said.

"It was beginning to get light. I went to Fleminggatan and collected his bag, which was already packed, and put it in Alfie's car. Then I came back here, cleaned up a bit and took the glasses and his coat, which was still hanging in the hall. I came back almost at once. I didn't dare stay and wait. So I took his car, drove to Arlanda and parked it there."

The man threw an appealing look at Martin Beck and said, "Everything went so easily, as if of its own accord. I put on the glasses, but the coat was too small. I carried it over my arm and went through the passport control. I don't remember much about the trip, but everything seemed just as simple."

"How had you planned to get away from there?"

"I just knew that it would work out somehow. I thought that the best way would be to take the train to the Austrian border and try to get over illegally. I had my own passport in my pocket and could return home from Vienna on that. I'd been there before, so I knew they didn't stamp the date of exit in your passport. But I was lucky again. I thought."

Martin Beck nodded.

"There was a shortage of rooms there and Alfie had been booked into two different hotels, just the first night at the one. I don't remember what it was called."

"The Ifjúság."

"Yes, maybe. Anyhow, I arrived there at the same time as a party of people speaking French. I gathered that they had come earlier the same day. They looked like students—several of the fellows had beards. When I turned in Alfie's—Matsson's passport, the porter was just sorting other passports into the pigeonholes. People who had already registered. I stayed on a moment in the vestibule and then when the porter stepped away for a minute, I got the chance to take one of those passports. I only had to look at three of them before I found one I thought was suitable—it was Belgian. The fellow was named Roederer or something like that. Anyway, the name reminded me of some kind of champagne.

Martin Beck looked carefully at his watch.

"And the next morning?"

"Then I was given back Alfie's—Matsson's passport and went to the other hotel. It was large and grand. The Duna, it was called. I handed in the passport, still Alfie's, at the reception desk and put his bag up in the room. I didn't stay longer than half an hour. Then I left. I'd got hold of a map and made my way to the railway station. On the way, I discovered I still had the room key in my pocket. It was large and a nuisance, so I threw it down outside a police station as I was walking past. I thought it was a good idea."

"Not especially," said Kollberg.

Gunnarsson smiled faintly.

"I managed to catch the express to Vienna and it took only four hours. First I took off Alfie's glasses, of course, and rolled up the coat. At that point I used the Belgian passport and that worked just as well. The train was very crowded and the passport officer was in a hurry. It was a girl, by the way. In Vienna, I took a taxi from the Eastern Railway Station directly to the airport and got on the afternoon plane to Stockholm."

"What did you do with Roeder's passport?" said Martin Beck.

"Tore it up and flushed the pieces down a toilet at the Eastern Railway Station. The glasses too. I smashed the glass and broke up the frames."

"And his coat?"

"I hung that up on a hook in the cafeteria on the station."

"And by the evening you were back here again?"

"Yes, I went up to the office then and handed in two articles I'd written earlier."

It was silent in the room. Finally Martin Beck said, "Did you try the bed?"

"Where?"

"At the Duna?"

"Yes. It creaked."

Gunnarsson looked down at his hands again. Then he said quietly, "I was in a very difficult situation. Not only for myself."

He looked quickly at the photograph.

"If nothing untoward had happened, I would have got married on Sunday. And . . ."

"Yes?"

"Actually it was an accident. Can you understand . . ."

"Yes," said Martin Beck.

Kollberg had hardly moved during the last hour. Now he suddenly shrugged his shoulders and said irritably, "O.K. Come on, let's go."

The man who had killed Alf Matsson suddenly sagged.

"Yes, of course," he said thickly. "I'm sorry."

He rose quickly and went out to the bathroom. Neither of the other two men moved, but Martin Beck looked unhappily at the closed door. Kollberg followed his look and said, "There's nothing in there he can hurt himself with. I've even taken away the toothbrush glass."

"There was a box of sleeping pills on the night table. Twenty-five in it, at least."

Kollberg went into the bedroom and came back.

"It's gone," he said.

He looked at the bathroom door.

"Shall we—"

"No," said Martin Beck. "We'll wait."

They did not need to wait more than thirty seconds. Åke Gunnarsson came out unbidden. He smiled weakly and said, "Can we go now?"

No one answered him. Kollberg went into the bathroom, got up on the toilet, lifted the lid of the tank, thrust his hand down and pulled out the empty pillbox. He read the label on it as he walked back into the study.

"Vesperax," he said. "A dangerous sort."

Then he looked at Gunnarsson and said in a troubled voice, "That was rather unnecessary, wasn't it? Now we've got to take you to the hospital. They'll put a bib on you which reaches all the way down to your feet and then they stick a rubber tube down your throat. Tomorrow you won't be able to eat or talk."

Martin Beck phoned for a radio car.

They walked swiftly down the stairs, all driven by the same wish to get away quickly.

The radio car was already there.

"Stomach-pump case," said Kollberg. "It's quite urgent. We'll follow you."

When Gunnarsson was already seated in the car, Kollberg seemed to remember something. He held the door open for a moment and said, "When you went from the hotel to the train, did you go to the wrong station at first?"

The man who had killed Alf Matsson looked at him with eyes that had already begun to look glazed and unnatural.

"Yes. How did you know that?"

Kollberg shut the door. The car drove away. The police-man at the wheel switched on the siren at the first corner.

Policemen in gray overalls were moving carefully among heaps of ash and charred beams on the site of the burnt-out house. A small group of Sunday walkers with baby carriages and pastry cartons had gathered outside the roped-off area and were staring inquisitively. It was already past four o'clock.

As soon as Martin Beck and Kollberg got out of the car, Stenström detached himself from a group of policemen and came over to them.

"You were right," he said. "He's in there, but there isn't much left of him."

An hour later they were again on their way into the city. As they passed the old city limit Kollberg said, "In a week the firm that is building there would have driven over it all with a bulldozer."

Martin Beck nodded.

"He did his best," said Kollberg philosophically. "And it wasn't that bad. If he'd known a little more about Matsson, and gone to the trouble of looking to see what was in the bag, and left the plane in Copenhagen instead of taking the risk of rubbing things out in his passport . . ."

He left the sentence unfinished. Martin Beck looked at him sideways.

"Then what? Do you mean he might have got away with it?"

"No," said Kollberg. "Of course not."

Despite the debatable summer weather, there were crowds of people at Vanadis Baths. As they passed it, Kollberg cleared his throat and said, "I don't see why you should go on with this any longer. Why, you're supposed to be on holiday."

Martin Beck looked at his watch. He would not have time to get out to the island today.

"You can drop me at Odengatan," he said.

Kollberg stopped in front of a movie theater on the corner.

"G'by, then," he said.

"Bye."

They did not even shake hands. Martin Beck stood on the pavement watching the car drive away. Then he walked diagonally across the street, around the corner and into a restaurant there, the Metropole. The lighting in the bar was subdued and pleasant and at one of the corner tables a low-keyed conversation was going on.

He sat down at the bar.

"Whisky," he said.

The barman was a large man with calm eyes, swift movements and a snow-white jacket.

"Icewater?"

"Yes, why not?"

"Right," said the barman. "Great. Double whisky with icewater. Can't be beat."

Martin Beck stayed on the bar stool for four hours. He did not speak again, but now and again pointed at his glass. The man in the white jacket did not say anything either. It was better that way.

Martin Beck looked at his own face in the smoky mirror behind the row of bottles. When the image began to blur, he called for a taxi and went home. He began to undress while he was still in the hall.

30

Martin Beck woke up with a start from a deep and dreamless sleep. The blanket and sheet had fallen to the floor and he was cold. When he got up to shut the balcony door, he saw stars before his eyes. His head thumped and his mouth felt stiff and dry. He went out into the bathroom and with difficulty swallowed two anodyne tablets, which he rinsed down with a tumbler of water. Then he went back to bed, pulled the sheet and blanket over him and tried to go back to sleep. After a couple hours half-sleep filled with nightmares, he got up and stood under the shower for a long time before dressing slowly. Then he went out onto the balcony and stood there with his elbows on the balcony rail, his chin in his hands.

The sky was high and clear and the cool morning air held an omen of autumn. For a while, he watched a fat dachshund leisurely making its way through the tree trunks in the little green arc outside the building. It was called a grove, but hardly lived up to its name. The ground between the evergreens was covered with pine needles and trash, and the little grass that had been there in the early summer had long since been trampled away.

Martin Beck went back into the bedroom and made his bed. Then he walked restlessly through the rooms for a while, putting a few trifles and books into his briefcase before leaving the flat.

He took the subway to the quay. The boat was not due to leave for an hour, so he strolled slowly along the quay toward the bridge. His boat was in and the gangway down: a couple of the crew were piling boxes on the foredeck. Martin Beck did not go on board but continued walking and then stopped for a cup of tea, which immediately made him feel even worse.

A quarter of an hour before the time of departure, he boarded the island boat, which had now got up steam and was belching white smoke out of its funnel. He went up on deck and sat in the same place he had sat when he had begun his holiday, scarcely two weeks ago. Now nothing would stop him completing it, he thought, but he no longer felt any pleasure or enthusiasm at the thought of his holiday or the island.

The engine thumped, the boat backed out, the whistle sounded out and Martin Beck leaned over the railing, staring down into the foaming whirlpools of water. The sense of a summer holiday was gone and he felt nothing but misery.

After a while, he went into the saloon and drank a mineral water. When he came out on deck again, his place had been taken by a fat, red-faced gentleman in a sportsuit and a beret.

Before Martin Beck had time to retreat, the fat man introduced himself and let loose a gushing stream of words on the beauty of the archipelago, which he knew intimately. Martin Beck listened apathetically while the man pointed out the islands they passed and gave their names. Finally managing to break off the one-sided conversation, Martin Beck fled to the aft saloon.

For the rest of the journey he lay in the half-light on one of the hard, plush-upholstered benches, looking at the dust swirling in the shaft of greenish light from the scuttle.

Nygren was sitting waiting in his motorboat at the steamer jetty. As they approached the island, he switched off the motor and let the boat glide past the little jetty so that Martin could jump ashore. Then he switched on the motor again, waved his hand and vanished around the point.

Martin Beck walked up to the cottage. His wife was lying in the lee behind the house, sunbathing naked on a blanket.

"Hi."

"Hi, I didn't hear you coming."

"Where are the kids?"

"Out with the boat."

"Oh."

"How was Budapest?"

"Very beautiful. Didn't you get the postcard I sent?"

"No."

"It'll come later, I suppose."

He went on into the cottage, drank a scoop of water and stood still, staring at the wall. He thought of the fair-haired woman with the chain necklace and wondered whether she had stood for a long time ringing the bell without anyone coming to open the door. Or whether she had come so late that the apartment had already been crawling with policemen with tweezers and cans of powder.

He heard his wife coming into the room.

"How are you, really?"

"Not well," said Martin Beck.

THE LOCKED ROOM

A woman robs a bank. A corpse is found shot through the heart in a room locked from within—no firearm in sight. To the eerily intuitive inspector Martin Beck, these two seemingly disparate cases are facets of the same puzzle. And solving it is of vital importance. Only by finding out what happened in the locked room can Beck—haunted by a near-fatal bullet wound and the demise of a soulless marriage—escape from an airtight prison of his own. From its classic premise, *The Locked Room* accelerates into an engrossing novel of the mind. Exploring the ramifications of egotism and intellect, luck and accident, and set against the backdrop of the inspired deductions and monstrous errors of Martin Beck and the Stockholm Homicide Squad, this tour de force of detection bears the unmistakable substance and gravity of real life.

Crime Fiction/978-0-679-74222-7

ROSEANNA

On a July afternoon, a young woman's body is dredged from Sweden's beautiful Lake Vättern. With no clues Beck begins an investigation not only to uncover a murderer but also to discover who the victim was. Three months later, all Beck knows is that her name was Roseanna and that she could have been strangled by any one of eighty-five people on a cruise. As the melancholic Beck narrows the list of suspects, he is drawn increasingly to the enigma of the victim, a free-spirited traveler with a penchant for casual sex, and to the psychopathology of a murderer with a distinctive—indeed, terrifying—sense of propriety. With its authentically rendered settings and vividly realized characters, and its command over the intricately woven details of police detection, *Roseanna* is a masterpiece of suspense and sadness.

Crime Fiction/978-0-307-39046-2

ALSO AVAILABLE FROM
VINTAGE CRIME/BLACK LIZARD

Henning Mankell's Kurt Wallander Mysteries:

FACELESS KILLERS

In a senselessly violent crime, an elderly farmer is bludgeoned to death in a remote Swedish farmhouse, and his wife is left to die with a noose around her neck. And as if this didn't present enough problems for the Ystad police inspector Kurt Wallander, the dying woman's last word is *foreign*, leaving the police the one tangible clue they have—and in the process, the match that could inflame Sweden's already smoldering anti-immigrant sentiments.

Crime Fiction/978-1-4000-3157-3

THE DOGS OF RIGA

On the Swedish coastline, two bodies, victims of grisly torture and cold execution, are discovered in a life raft. With no witnesses, no motives, and no crime scene, Wallander is frustrated and uncertain he has the ability to solve a case as mysterious as it is heinous. Wallander thinks his work is done when the case is taken up by the Riga police in Latvia, but then he is suddenly called in to assist on the case.

Crime Fiction/978-1-4000-3152-8

THE WHITE LIONESS

When Wallander is called in to investigate the execution-style murder of a Swedish housewife, it initially seems like a routine case. But when the prime suspect's alibi turns out to be airtight, Wallander must look deeper into the case, and soon uncovers an assassination plot while also finding himself entangled with the secret police and a KGB agent.

Crime Fiction/978-1-4000-3155-9

SIDETRACKED

The former minister of justice has been murdered, and Wallander is frantic to track down the killer before he strikes again. But his investigation is beset with obstacles—a distracted department, a long-distance relationship with a murdered policeman's widow, and his unshakably haunting preoccupation with a young girl who he witnessed committing suicide.

Crime Fiction/978-1-4000-3156-6

THE FIFTH WOMAN

In an African convent, four nuns and a unidentified fifth woman are brutally murdered. A year later in Sweden, Wallander is baffled and appalled by two murders. A retired car dealer is impaled on sharpened bamboo poles in a ditch behind his secluded home, and the body of a missing florist is discovered—strangled and tied to a tree. What ensues is a case that will test Wallander's strength and patience, because in order to discover the reason behind these murders, he will need to uncover an elusive connection between these deaths and the earlier unsolved murder in Africa of the fifth woman.

Crime Fiction/978-1-4000-3154-2

ONE STEP BEHIND

On Midsummer's Eve, three role-playing teens dressed in eighteenth-century garb are shot in a secluded Swedish meadow. When one of Inspector Wallander's most trusted colleagues—someone whose help he hoped to rely on to solve the crime—also turns up dead, he knows the murders are related. Reeling from his father's death and facing his own deteriorating health, Wallander tracks the lethal progress of the killer.

Crime Fiction/978-1-4000-3151-1

FIREWALL

A body is found at an ATM, the apparent victim of heart attack. Then two teenage girls are arrested for the brutal murder of a cab driver. At first these two incidents seem to have nothing in common, but as Wallander delves deeper into the mystery of why the girls murdered the cab driver he begins to unravel a plot much more involved than he initially suspected. The two cases become one and lead to a conspiracy that stretches outside Sweden.

Crime Fiction/978-1-4000-3153-5

THE MAN WHO SMILED

A lawyer driving home at night stops to investigate an effigy in the middle of the highway. The lawyer is hit over the head and dies. Within a week the lawyer's son is also killed. The prime suspect is a powerful corporate mogul with a gleaming smile that Wallander believes hides the evil glee of a killer. As Wallander uncovers the truth, the murderers begin closing in on him.

Crime Fiction/978-1-4000-9583-4

THE RETURN
An Inspector Van Veeteren Mystery
by Håkan Nesser

On a rainy April day, a body—or what is left of it—is found by a young girl. Wrapped in a blanket, the corpse has no hands, feet, or head, and it signals the work of a brutal, methodical killer. The victim, Leopold Verhaven, was a track star before he was convicted of killing two of his ex-lovers. He consistently proclaimed his innocence, however, and was killed on the day of his return to society. This latest murder is more than a little perplexing, and Chief Inspector Van Veeteren is determined to discover the truth, even if it means taking the law into his own hands.

Crime Fiction/978-1-4000-3033-0

VINTAGE CRIME/BLACK LIZARD
Available at your local bookstore, or visit
www.randomhouse.com